THE PERSISTENCE OF MEMORY

and

OTHER STORIES

Praise for *Heaven, Indiana*

In *Heaven, Indiana* magical realism comes to the heartland…Jan Maher expertly and effortlessly manipulates this timeless place and this place-full time into a rich amalgam of a novel. *Heaven, Indiana* is out of this world and so much of it.

—Michael Martone, author, *The Moon over Wapakoneta: Fictions and Science Fictions from Indiana and Beyond*

A lush, multilayered portrait of the cycle of life. This is a remarkable piece of writing.

—Arthur C. Jones, author, *Wade in the Water: The Wisdom of the Spirituals*

Maher's work is deeply embedded in the women's literary tradition of friendship and mother-daughter stories, richly evocative, both rooted and visionary.

—Susan Koppelman, editor, *Between Mothers and Daughters: Stories Across a Generation* (The Women's Stories Project)

A story of crossed paths, of roads not taken, a leaving and a homecoming. This little bit of Heaven leaves us wanting more.

—Wendy Fawthrop, *Seattle Union Record*

A funny, poignant tale of an imperfect paradise.

—*Kirkus Reviews* (Starred)

Praise for *Earth As It Is*

A quietly luminous tale of folksy gender-bending that's entertaining and authentic.

—*Kirkus Reviews (Starred)*

A satisfyingly complex character study exploring gender identity in the postwar Midwest…the story is transportive.

—*Publishers Weekly*

Both loving and heartbreaking, *Earth As It Is* lends a new perspective to an ongoing dialogue.

—*Foreword Reviews*

A superbly crafted novel by an exceptionally skillful storyteller, *Earth As It Is* reveals author Jan Maher's genuine flair for a fully engaging originality.

—*Midwest Review of Books*

ALSO BY JAN MAHER

Heaven, Indiana
Earth As It Is

THE
PERSISTENCE
OF MEMORY

and

OTHER STORIES

JAN MAHER

DOG HOLLOW PRESS

Published by Dog Hollow Press
38 Forest Avenue
Greenfield, MA 01301

The Persistence of Memory and Other Stories

Print ISBN: 978-1-943547-04-3
Digital ISBN: 978-1-943547-05-0

Library of Congress Control Number: 2020902207

www.doghollowpress.com

Cover design: Robin Locke Monda

"A Real Prince" first appeared in *Meat for Tea: The Valley Review*, Volume 10/4

"Livia's Daddy Comes Home from the War" first appeared in *A Flash of Words: 49 Flash Fiction Stories*, Scout Media, January 11, 2019

"Vitae" first appeared online at *Writes for All*, Volume 1/3. 2011, http://www.writesforall.com

"Ashes to Ashes" first appeared in *Third Wednesday*, summer, 2011

"Dancing in the Dark" first appeared in *A Contract of Words: 27 Short Stories*, Scout Media, April 1, 2018

"Fencing" first appeared in *Meat for Tea: The Valley Review*, Volume 10/4

"Half Full" first appeared in *Atticus Review*, atticusreview.org, January 13, 2014

"Turn, Turn, Turn" first appeared in *Persimmon Tree*, persimmontree.org, Fall 2010.

"The Persistence of Memory" first appeared in *Ride 2: More Short Fiction about Bicycles*, Typeflow, January 11, 2013

Editorial consultant: Ann B. Tracy

Contents

A Real Prince

YANKA STIRRED THE ashes in the stove, poking for hot embers. In the icy cold of pre-dawn winter, her fingers were stiff as sticks and her body shook. She was hoping to find a live coal. It would make starting the fire up so much easier. By her side lay a small pile of dried grass and twigs, next to a few larger chunks of firewood. She found the ember she was seeking and made a small noise of satisfaction. Carefully, she lifted the all-but-dead ashes from the firebox and dropped the shovelful into the ash bucket. Then she placed the grass and twigs atop the glowing coal, and blew gently and noisily on the smoldering pile. When it burst into full flame she chortled and put a small bit of firewood on the pile, then a second piece, crosswise to the first. She let it all burn for a moment, to be sure it wouldn't be going out, then added a third piece. Waited for it to catch, and layered on the fourth. Each piece placed as carefully as if it were crystal for the table.

This was Yanka's favorite time of day. The transition from frigid cold to the blazing warmth provided by the fire enchanted her. While it was still starting, before anyone else would be up to order her about, she liked to sit on her haunches, hunkering on the hearth, and see how close she could put her fingers without burning them.

Soon enough she would have to leave the fire and begin hauling water to the kitchen. Today, it would be ice to haul: big frozen chunks that would have to be melted before the water was useable.

She didn't like the cold.

She might have told her keepers so, but Yanka never spoke. When she made sounds they were guttural, throaty, inarticulate. She expressed pleasures and pains clearly enough though. No one was ever in doubt as to where her feelings stood.

When she despaired, her anguish touched others in places they scarcely knew existed. When she was completely delighted she laughed a low hearty chuckle that inspired the dourest person to smile in empathy.

It was entirely irregular that she'd even been allowed to live, given her obvious deficits. It was rumored that she was the daughter of a very high-ranking Official, and so had been left with Cook to be raised as a servant girl instead of being terminated like any of the others who showed such problems. Since she was so easy going, and they wouldn't have dared to, anyway, no one at the Outpost complained.

After she had completed her chores for the day, Yanka was permitted to sit at the back of the Children's Circle and listen to the stories they learned. She took great joy in this, and stored in her secret self all the images of ugly trolls, clever elves, evil stepmothers, wily wolves, brave woodchoppers, exquisite princesses, and imperious kings she ever heard.

Her favorite stories were the ones in which the dull-witted but kind-hearted third sons won the hands of princesses in marriage. Yanka allowed herself, once in a while, to imagine the scene in which a handsome prince who could marry anyone he wanted would choose her above all others. Fortunately, her lack of speech kept this a private vision, for it would not have been heard charitably.

Yanka wasn't sure what a real prince looked like. In her world there were Governesses, Cooks, Children, and Wenches. She'd heard of Athletes, Scholars, Counselors, Officials, Soldiers, and Enemies. And, of course, of the Princes and

Princesses who resided in her favorite stories, as examples to the youngest ones of something Governess called Moral Order.

On this particular day when the children gathered for their learning circle, Yanka noticed that Governess was upset. She was impatient with the little ones, and sarcastic with the older children. When they finally settled down she spoke to them with a grim expression that belied the content of her speech.

"Children," she said, "We are about to be greatly honored. Our Soldiers are coming to stay here. They are on their way to battle the Enemy. We must treat them with great respect: whatever they want for their comfort and pleasure it is our glad duty to provide them."

Then she spoke directly to Yanka, who was hunkered in the nearby corner, for the first time Yanka could remember. "You will need to bring in more water, so they can bathe. And keep the fire going all night long. You will have to sleep by the fire."

Yanka nodded, ecstatic. To sleep by the fire! To feed its dancing flames all night long! It would be more than enough to make up for the extra trips hauling ice. She couldn't quite picture Soldiers, never having seen them before, but having heard stories of them vanquishing Enemies, she was excited, anticipating something wonderful.

Then Governess turned to the oldest girls in the circle. "Those of you who would have become Wenches in another year or two will have your status confirmed ahead of time. You are to be at the service of our Soldiers. You will serve them food and drink. You will share their beds when asked to. You must keep your bodies clean and fresh at all times."

The twelve- and thirteen-year-old girls looked smugly at the younger children. This would be the end of their lives in the Children's Circle. They would be part of the important world of adults from now on.

When the Soldiers came the small community exploded with activity. The Soldiers liked to sing and drink and grab the Wenches by their budding breasts and round firm buttocks. They stayed for three nights, drilling by day, guzzling and carousing by night. On the third night the tall one with the hawk-like nose got a notion to give Yanka some grog. "Go ahead. Drink it down, Idiot Girl. Maybe it'll bring some sense to you." The Soldiers all laughed and Yanka laughed too. She downed the cup lustily, like she'd seen them do. They cheered and gave her another. After five cups of grog, Yanka's head was swimming. The Soldiers began to sing, and the sharp-nosed one commanded Yanka to dance. Yanka had never been told to dance before but she'd seen the Wenches dance. She began to sway and thrust her hips in imitation. The Soldiers roared their approval. Yanka buckled and swayed, heavy with grog and heady with the attention of the Soldiers. They began to push her from one to another, spinning her as she lurched around, fighting to maintain her balance. She saw their eyes flash by in the blur—blue eyes, gray eyes, brown eyes, green eyes. She landed, at the end of their song, in the arms of Hawk Nose who announced, "Bedtime, Soldiers."

Abruptly, he let go of her and she thudded to the floor. "Let's go, Pretty Ones," he said, beckoning the Wenches, and they all filed out to their sleeping quarters, leaving Yanka in a heap.

With considerable effort, she pulled herself up and managed to get to the privy to relieve her bladder. The chance to urinate cleared her head a bit and she remembered her duty to keep the fire going. On her way back she stopped for more firewood so that she would not have to go out in the cold again before morning.

The green-eyed Soldier was there when she got back. He

was squatting by the fire, holding his hands out to warm them. Yanka took it as a rebuke and hurried over to stoke the blaze. As the flames rose, the green-eyed Soldier spoke.

"Feels good," he said. Yanka made a throaty, agreeable sound. She, too, held her hands out to warm them.

Green Eyes seized them in his own. "Yanka," he whispered, "I'm sorry. We shouldn't have treated you that way."

Yanka stared in wonder at the young man's face. She saw a look there she'd never seen before.

"You're a good soul," Green Eyes went on. "You deserve better. When the War is over I'll see what I can do for you."

Yanka looked at him, uncomprehending.

"I'll try to come back, to see how you are. Don't tell anyone I spoke to you," he added needlessly, for Yanka couldn't have even had she wanted to.

The next day the Soldiers marched off into the forest.

The day after, when Yanka got to the river to cut ice, she found Green Eyes, Hawk Nose and all the others frozen stiff, bloody and blue on the icy banks, victims of an ambush. Yanka cried out, dropped her bucket, and ran blubbering back to the village. Cook was angry at first, then realized there was trouble. She rounded up all the adults in the compound and they went down to the river.

Yanka still had to cut the ice and bring it back. The rest carried corpses to be buried. As they made their way slowly through the trees, the Wenches talked quietly among themselves, so they would not be heard criticizing Soldiers. Yanka trudged beside them, lugging ice. "I'm not sorry," breathed one.

"Nor I," whispered another.

"Except this one," the third said softly, referring to Green Eyes, whose feet she carried. The Wench at his head agreed.

"Yes, he was a real prince. Not like the others."

Yanka understood now. That's why he was so different. So difficult to understand. He was a Real Prince. And he had spoken to her kindly, even held her hand!

"Yes," whispered the third. "You don't see a fellow like that very often. A man like him comes along once in a hundred years."

Once in a hundred years, thought Yanka, and she smiled a slow smile of delight. He would come back like he said he would.

All she had to do was wait a hundred years.

Livia's Daddy Comes Home from the War

MAMA'S ACTING FUNNY. It's not Sunday, and she makes me and Jed put on Sunday clothes. And I have to put my paper dolls away, and just sit on the davenport and look at my picture book. And Jed has to comb his hair. Mama tucks his shirt in and he asks why and she says someone special is going to be here. And there's a knock and she says he's here and a man walks into the room in funny clothes. His shirt and pants are muddy color, and a hat like none I ever seen. It's the same color too. Greeny brown. And she kisses him. The only time I ever seen her kiss a man was New Year's Eve they hung a thing in the doorway and my Uncle Jake standed under it and they made us all kiss him, even Gramma kissed him and my cousin Lucy who is more little than me. I'm almost five and she's three and a brat. She kisses him a long one. He acts like he doesn't see me or Jed till that's over. Then he sticks his hand out to Jed like he's grownup or something even though he's nine and a pain and says hi son how ya doing.

Jed gets red and shuffles his feet. He says fine so quiet I almost can't hear him say it and Mama just smiles like it's Christmas which it isn't it's the day before my birthday. I'm almost five and Christmas was before Easter.

And Jed shakes his hand. And then he asks me can he have a kiss. I'm not spose to kiss people I don't know. I'm looking at his feet and not his eyes. I watched his eyes when he shaked Jake's hand. His eyes are crinkly and I don't like that. Livia, Mama says, Livia, it's your daddy come home from the war you can kiss him hello, he's your daddy. He's home now.

I chew on the inside part of my lip and I look up at his crinkly-eyed old face and I say loud that isn't my daddy. He doesn't look like that. He doesn't wear them funny clothes. Then Jed hits me on the head with his knuckles and it hurts so I kick him but he gets away. Dummy he says. That's just his uniform. That's just your uniform, ain't it Dad Jed says with a stupid grin just cause he thinks he's hot stuff just cause he's four years older.

Mama says Jed keep your hands off your sister and the man laughs ho ho ho like them Santa Clauses they got at Christmas at all the stores and I don't think they are really Santa Clauses cause there's only one of him. And he's sposed to be making things. This man here laughs like that and Mama says you probly don't member him you were just a baby when he went overseas. Nu uh, I was one, I say and besides my daddy's in France I say. I stick my lip out cause I know I'm right. He sent me shoes for Easter and I pull my dress up to show them.

He says they are pretty and I can tell he never seen them before. If you never seen them before you can't be my daddy I say. Mama, I say, he can't be my daddy. I showed it.

She's pretty smart he says and Jed says smart mouth dumb head and Mama says shut up Jed. I sent your mama money, he says, and she got you the shoes. I stick my lip out at Mama you said my shoes came from my daddy in France. Mama says the money came from France and I say you said the *shoes* came from France and then I am quiet. I'm thinking what other lies did she tell me? Do you want to see some French money he says and he puts his hand in his pocket and pulls out two things like pennies and he gives me one and Jed one.

Then Jed goes jumping on him did you bring me anything from the war he says. Ho ho ho says the man, what sort of things do you want? A gun Jed says. Ho ho ho they don't let you take guns home from the war. You can have my canteen. Where is it Jed yells. I'll get it for you in a minute he ho ho's. First I want a hug from my Livia. I'm not your Livia I say.

Ho ho ho, come here a minute the man says I'll let you wear my hat and he puts the greeny brown thing on my head. I throw it on the floor. Then Jed says can I have it Daddy and the man looks at it and looks at me and looks at Jed and looks at me and Jed goes to pick it up and I grab it. No he says J-boy, the hat is for Livia. I want my canteen says Jed can you get it now?

Yes I'll get it now he says and turns away from looking at me.

I'm membering hard now looking at his back but I can't member about this man. I member a man in France who sended me shoes but now I can't member what he's sposed to look like. He puts his hand in his big greeny brown bag and pulls out another greeny brown thing that's round. Everything about him is greeny brown. Here you go, J-boy, you can keep this. Use it if you ever go fishing or camping. Jed says can I have the hat too, Daddy? Please? Livia don't want it.

I hold the hat with both my hands. The man says no J-boy, I'll find you some other things. First I want to get out of these clothes. Don't ever want to wear them again, he says.

Why not Daddy, Jed's looking at him funny and Mama is too, different from Jed. Mama's crying, I know cause I can see her face is wet. I never seen her cry before.

Cause the war is over, the man says. I don't ever want to fight another one.

Not ever says Jed isn't war fun?

The man gets a funny look on his face too and Mama says you go play now J-boy. Daddy's going to change into see villyun clothes.

What's that, says Jed.

Like what you're wearing, says the man. Just regular clothes. I don't ever want to wear these ugly things again.

Well, just there he knows they're ugly. I'm glad he knows that. He looks at me again and says after I get my clothes changed I want you to tell me what you want for your birthday tomorrow. He knows that too! Maybe he is my daddy. I'm not sure now. I sure don't member him like this. Then he goes into my mama's bedroom, with his big greeny brown bag. She goes in too, and she shuts the door. Jed goes into the kitchen and puts water in the round thing.

I watch Mama's door and practice saying to myself my Daddy's home from the war.

My Daddy's home from the war.

Vitae

Was't Dionysus made men mad for gold?
Lust lured them to this Hell carved i' the cold.
Athena's wiser ways the seekers lost,
While on Poseidon's frozen seas their tos't
And twisted frames once young, in brief, grew old
Among the Heathen under stars yet crossed,
Their bones eternal lovers to the frost.
I have not heart to hear another's breath.
Adonis turned to ice. Calumny! Death!
The Heavens part, the Father calls us: was't
The failure of such men His word to heed
That led them to their graveyard made of Greed?
    ~ SARAH PETITBOIS CRUMM (1852)

THE SEVERANCE PACKAGE covered Dr. Sally Agnew for a quarter, and unemployment for the rest of the year, during which she sent out 213 cover letters with her curriculum vitae and worked on her book: *The Poetry of Sarah Petibois Crumm: An Alaskan Pioneer Woman's Metaphors.* At least when former colleagues asked what she was doing, that's what she told them. At first it was true. A year off with pay was the proverbial golden opportunity to finish her magnum opus. As the weeks had worn by, she'd written less and pondered more. In three month's time, she'd moved to the southeast quadrant of the city where she was sure she would never see another academic. Once away from the well-intentioned inquiries about her work, a profound ennui seized her and she stopped even pretending to write.

The university life was supposed to have been her meal ticket in perpetuity. Earning her degree as she did, *summa cum laude*, garnered her several offers. She'd taken the one that provided the best salary and the cushiest teaching load: mostly grad students, a handful of advisees. "What the hell do you do to earn all that money," her father had rasped from his hospital bed when she first told him. He'd worked in a foundry all his life and was dying of a rare lung disease. "That's some crazy business, people paying you to read poetry," he told her. Nonetheless, he was pleased that this spoiled princess child of his was finally, after two decades of the best schools he couldn't afford, going to be able to support herself. His illness, after his wife's terminal cancer the year before, had left him with nothing by way of an estate. Sally would have to stand on her own two feet.

"It's tenure track, too," she told her dad. "Once you get tenure, they can't fire you."

That was five years ago. A year later, her father died. Four years after that, two short of tenure, the economy followed.

Was it any wonder she'd been the one they let go when the university got word the budget would be cut fifteen per cent and each department was expected to share in the burden? They even cut one of the football coaches, so it would stretch credulity to expect them keep a specialized scholar like her. Save a single section of Comp 101, Nineteeth Century Alaskan Women's Poetry and Introduction to Etymology were all she'd ever taught, all she ever expected to teach. Mindful of the drastic economy and falling enrollment in her corner of the graduate programs, she'd come to that last meeting with the department head prepared to humble herself and accept

a second section of Freshman Comp, even though the eigh-
teen- and nineteen year-olds intimidated her with their frank
lack of interest in the minutiae that comprised her career and
mental life.

"If you could teach four sections of Business English for
non-majors..." the department head had stared wistfully
over her head, tapping the blunt end of his pen against his
teeth, then admonishing himself before she could consider an
answer. "Of course not. You'd go mad, Sally, and besides, Dr.
Fordhammer can take that on. I've got to do something with
him because he's tenured. I'm so sorry," he concluded, running
his craggy fingers through a white mane of hair, dislodging a
flurry of dandruff that reminded her of Christmas decorative
scenes encased in plastic and water, with snowflakes that fell
when the entire tiny scene was turned upside down and right
side up again. "We're losing a great asset. I'm sure, though,
with your credentials, you'll land on your feet."

She'd left analyzing the metaphor: she was a cat fond of its
cozy ivory tower window ledge where it is used to surveying
the world below. A cat who does not choose to jump, and yet
has found itself hurtling toward the pavement below. A cat
who has, in fact, been pushed. Her life as a crime scene. And
yet a cat who will survive, albeit on possibly shattered ankles
and most certainly sore feet.

Indeed, she would survive, she told herself. Her book
could be a unique contribution to the literature. Alas, the
book refused to let itself be written. Sarah Petibois Crumm's
allusions to Greek mythology notwithstanding, the crux of
Crumm's poetry was that men died cold miserable deaths
from greed and the women they partnered with were left
behind to cope as best they could. It wasn't really a metaphor
for anything. It was simply life. Crumm's grizzlies steadfastly

remained hairy brown beasts. Blood on snow was just that. "Cruel mountains as Olympus crowned with white/gaze down on rigid snow where crimson blood/of brave but mortal pioneers doth flood/and in chill winter's pale and ghostly light/ the caribou and grizzly in their might/o'er victims of their flesh and fang they stood/and churned the bones of fathers into mud…" This was not literary device. This was simple harsh fact.

She began to doubt too, who, after all, her scholarly efforts would actually benefit. With luck, her book might be adopted by a few graduate departments large enough to have such deliciously specialized classes. Perhaps one or two PhD candidates would give a rat's ass about these desperate women who kept themselves from going stark raving in the endless Alaskan wilderness winters by writing third rate sonnets. All this assuming she could even find a publisher in these disastrous times.

Disastrous: from the Greek "aster," meaning stars. Ill-fated times.

As the end of her benefits drew near, she became as resourceful as those staunch pioneer poets. She gave up the laundromat in favor of washing her clothes in the bathtub with bits of hand soap filched from public restrooms (she carried a wash cloth with her at all times, in a Ziploc® bag, and impregnated it with the liquid soap). Public restrooms were also her source of toilet paper: her large handbag could easily hold three or four ends of rolls. It was a far cry from being paid handsomely for teaching about pioneer poet women making do with harsh lye handmade soaps and old rags for menstrual cycles. Though she did feel closer to them now, these subjects of her scholarly studies, than ever she had in the confines of the national archives. All those years she'd taught about them, droning on about hardship and endurance, but it was only now she felt she was even beginning to truly understand them. She gave up her high-priced Internet connection and became a regular at the branch library. There, through free public access, she stopped looking for meaning beyond the surface and turned her attention to amusing herself by translating and retranslating Crumm's words into various combinations of Greek, German, Russian, and French, using an online translating program. Then she would translate back again.

"The Children cling to prayers, they wail and weep/and fear to lay themselves abed to sleep" put to German, thence to French, thence Greek, and finally back to English became the enigmatic "The children persist in requests, the jammern [aytoes] and pleurent/et the fear in order to they put in abed, he sleeps." It passed the time. Just as it must have passed the time for Sarah Crumm to pen her modest sonnets after a day of salting fish, drying berries, and shooting wildlife.

Meanwhile, her cake of irony—for such she considered the situation she was enduring—had this to frost it: after the last check cleared, she would no longer be in the ranks of the unemployed. The statistics only counted the ones who still had benefits. From the Latin benefactum. Sounded a bit like the brand name of an individual piece of something good for the digestive tract. Which would become, perforce, a small piece of shit.

Thus it was that in a rather ugly, depressed, and frankly associative state of mind that she saw the sign: Now Hiring.

Now. Nu nun num. Hiring. Hyr. Hiren, hyrian. An old set of words. Exchanging wages for labor. In the present.

She took it as an omen. Stepped inside and asked for an application. The kid behind the counter was surprised. "You sure you want to work here?"

"Is there something wrong with working here?"

"It's bad hours," the pimply youth replied, slathering tomato sauce on an unbaked crust. "The shift that's open is the closing one."

Though she savored the oxymoronic sentence, the opening in closing, she did not get the job.

The unemployed construction worker who did lasted three days, then died in a holdup. The murderer made off with the man's credit cards, but no cash. He hadn't read the warning that the counter people had no access to the till. He couldn't read.

Nanza Pizza's take for the day remained safe in the lock box bolted under the counter, where it would stay until the day manager arrived after breakfast to trade the cash box for an empty one. The day manager carried a gun and let no one come between him and his responsibility to turn over the till to the owner, whose office was protected by a doorman who knew everyone who had business in the building by name, purpose, and habit; a personal secretary who could turn a man to a pillar of salt with her formidable glare; and should those two lines of defense fail, a locked office door with a .45 in the top drawer of the desk.

The sign appeared again the next morning, even as the cleaning crew was finishing scrubbing down all the surfaces sullied by the previous night's crime. She waited for the door to be unlocked. "I'm still interested," she told the kid.

"You're crazy, lady," he told her.

"Maybe," she said.

He shrugged. "Whatever."

His name was Tooley, and it fell to him to train her, his second training of the week, and fourth of the month. It was that kind of job.

Not that it required much training. Thought had been carefully removed from the equation. Everything was pre-measured, straight from the parent company came packets of cheese, sauce, and toppings, scientifically designed to eliminate waste and theft. No counter clerk could add a little extra mozzarella to a buddy's pie, let alone take even a small cheese, no toppings home without logging it and paying full price.

Apparently, she thought, desperate times call for precise measures.

Her first four weeks passed astonishingly uneventfully. She baked the pies, doled out the slices, ran the credit cards, took nothing larger than a twenty and watched the ultra-modern cash register, with its iron-clad security, mete out just the exact change needed, but only after it had been fed the proper bills, taken them into its jaws, peered at their details, and determined their legitimacy.

Legitimacy. An interesting word. A form of legitimate. Legit, I mate. I marry legitimacy. It wasn't the Greek, Latin, or Old English meaning, but it was what had begun to happen to her mind this past month. Her propensity to analyze had taken a turn for the puns and word plays embedded in just about everything she read and heard, and especially the words of her internal monologues.

It was inevitable in this place, as it was the only food-serving establishment in the neighborhood open past ten o'clock, that eventually there would be another holdup attempt by another fellow made illiterate whether by emotional tension, insufficient and/or ineffective schooling, or drastically compromised eyesight. This fellow was olive-skinned and handsome, and he didn't shift back and forth on his feet the way the coke addicts did, nor did he squint behind dark glasses worn even at midnight the way heroin addicts did. He stood still, and leaned

into the Plexiglass hole — the new one, that had replaced the
one our earlier desperado had shot through to make his lethal
point with the unemployed construction worker who, fortunately, had been married to his wife for eleven years which
meant she was able to collect survivor benefits based mostly
on what had once been a reasonable income.

He leaned in and in a quiet, urgent voice twinged with a
Greek accent demanded to have the contents of the till. Unlike
the construction worker, who had offended the previous thief
by asking "Can't you read?" she smiled brightly and replied in
what she hoped could pass for modern Greek, one of five lan-
guages she'd added to her repertoire through her compulsive
noodling on BabelFish.

Her classical Greek was flawless, but her attempt to sound
contemporary was pitiful: poorly accented, and though ade-
quately conjugated, excruciatingly inaccurate with regard to
vocabulary choices. He understood but a few words. Athens.
Sorry. Please.

"Speak English," he commanded and she complied, leaving
out the lament that she had yet to visit his home country —
hers too, if you counted a great-grandfather whose only
contribution to the family tree was his sperm and surname.

"I would give you every cent here if I could, but they don't
trust me. When I put money in here," she pointed to the cash
register, "it goes down here," she pointed to the lock box below.
"I'm sorry, but no one can get it out until tomorrow. Do you
want the money in my purse? I have about ten dollars. Please
take it if you wish."

"Ten dollars is nothing." The young man looked at her with
ill-disguised contempt. "I need four hundred for the rent."

"Do you want my job?"

That gave him pause. (Paws she thought, as she said the

phrase to herself. Like a little squirrel or a cat, padding in on little feet like the fog...)

"Excuse me, but I don't understand."

"My job. It pays minimum wage plus tips, but I must warn you the only tip I've ever gotten here was that I shouldn't have even applied for it. In two weeks you can make $400.00.

"It's dangerous, this job."

"Yes, yes it is. People like you come in with guns and overdue rent to pay." Her mind heard it as "toupee." What would an overdue rent toupee look like? Mussed up, no doubt. Perhaps a tad askew.

"I'm sorry. I don't want to hurt you."

She forced herself back to the rather perilous moment at hand. "I know. Tell you what. My take-home is $200 a week. My rent is $300. You wait with me till I close up, you come with me to my cash machine and I can take out $300 tonight. Come again tomorrow and stay with me during my shift and I'll take out another hundred. Keep me company every night and I'll go fifty-fifty with you."

He stared at her.

"And put the gun away," she advised. "There's a customer coming in."

He tucked the gun out of sight.

"I'll be with you in just a minute," she assured the newcomer. "There's one more thing," she said to the befuddled thief. "You teach me to speak modern Greek, and I'll teach you to read English."

"You are one crazy bitch," he told her.

"Yes," she agreed, leaning forward into the Plexiglass and staring him in the eye, "but I always land on my feet."

He turned and ran.

"Was that guy bothering you?" The man next at the counter

was not someone she'd seen before. A couple of years younger than she, dreads, green eyes, brown leather jacket, sinewy. His computer bag, slung over a shoulder, was well-made of heavy canvas but frayed at corners.

"Not really," she said, though her voice quavered and her hands shook. It was true. Pressed to put a verb to what had just happened, Sally would have to say he had not so much bothered her as awakened her. She'd been frightened, yes, but she had prevailed. There was no blood on the walls.

"Is it okay if I sit here for a while with my laptop?" he asked after ordering. "I've got finals coming up and it's too loud to concentrate at my place."

"Be my guest," she told him, sliding his pizza slices to him. She glanced at the volume he held. *J. Alfred Prufrock on the Montana Frontier.* "Is that a good book?"

"It's pretty interesting actually. The author ties together phrases from Eliot's poem with diaries from homesteaders the year Prufrock was published, then contextualizes it in terms of today's pulp mill industry in Montana." There was a graduate-student glow on his face as he warmed to his subject. "Oh, do not ask what is it?" he quoted, an energized, almost maniacal grin on his face. "A perfect motto for a pulp mill, don't you think? It's actually sort of a break-out book because for some crazy reason Oprah stumbled across it and decided she liked it."

It got Sally to thinking. Maybe there was a book to write after all. She could do it. She could. And with Sarah Palin in the news so much these days, who knows? Maybe she could tap into that whole Alaskan-frontier-infatuated market. Yes, forget the metaphors. Forget the ivory-tower analysis and the pretentious literary allusions. She'd take a whole different approach. *Grizzlies in Pizza Parlors: Real Life Lessons from the Poetry of Sarah Pettibois Crumm.* Blood on the snow, blood on the pizza parlor walls. Wolves on the tundra, wolves at the door. Victims of flesh and fang, victims of Wall Street.

For the first time in a year, she felt alive. Unconsciously, she shifted her weight, to soothe her aching feet.

Ashes to Ashes

GLORIOUS DIRT. CLUMPS of compost, ash, half-rotted leaves. I'm on my hands and knees chopping up weed roots. I like to be close to the processes: the decomposing, the sprouting, the leafing out, the blossoming, the fruit set, the harvest, and after the eating, the composting again. It's the first hours of the first warm day of spring. After eight years in this land of black flies and mosquitoes, I've learned to take advantage of opportunity. By tomorrow morning, insects will have hatched out by the thousands. By tomorrow afternoon, they will attack me mercilessly. Today, I will plant.

First the peas, pressing each wrinkled globe into its own loamy nest. The trick to peas, I have learned, is to run twine on both sides of the row so the vines will be supported no matter which direction they decide to roam.

It has taken several seasons, but I have finally fallen in love with this land. Last year, I filled the freezer with tomato sauce and ratatouille. This year, the dwarf pear I put in will bear fruit. The rhubarb will be robust enough to make a pie. And the peas will grow straight and tall. It helps, especially since Will was not granted tenure.

He finds me resting from my efforts at the end of the pea row. "Start packing," he calls from the back porch. "They offered me the position in Tucson. I start June first!"

"June first? Not September?"

"That's right. Not only that," Will says. "I stopped by the college to post a for rent notice and ran into the Baileys."

The Baileys. We went to dinner at their house the first fall we were here. Everything in place. Every blade of grass the perfect hue, the ideal length. Nary a weed in sight. Little signs all over, warning of pesticides. A poisonous lawn, a stupefyingly tidy home. "And…?"

"And they want to buy the place."

"This place?"

"Their daughter is getting a divorce and moving back to town. They're buying it for her. We met her, remember?"

"I remember. She's the one who made us take our shoes off at the door and told us how many microbes are in a square inch of dirt, how much dust the average person tracks inside during the course of a year."

"Well," Will says grinning impishly, "she'll be living here. And you can stop the planting process, because we'll have to reseed the whole area anyway: that's the only condition of sale. So the new grass gets established by June. I'll give a call right now to get that set up. They gave me the name of the folks who maintain their lawn. I was beginning to wonder," he continues, "if we'd ever get out of this Podunk town. Seems like the stars are finally aligned for good things to happen."

He disappears from the porch as cheerfully as he first materialized.

I dig a deeper trench now. Next to the peas that I've just unwittingly consigned to sure death by Weed 'n' Seed.

At my father's funeral, the men cut their ties to acknowledge their grief. I take my shears and lop the buttons off my gardening jacket. Four bright brassy circles fall to the ground. I press each one deep into the yielding earth, wet with spilling saltwater, and say Kaddish.

Dancing in the Dark

"Hold the elevator!"

Oh, God, she recognizes that voice. Victor, no doubt about it. The imperious tone, the expectation that the world revolves around him like all he has to do is issue the command and any reasonable person would jump to it. No, Claire will not hold the doors for him. Will not lunge on his command for the button. But the other woman in the elevator does. She can afford to. She hasn't been married to the creep for more than a decade. Claire sees him now, huffing across the lobby. Once assured the elevator is being held, he slows to a breathless amble, too self-centered to realize that people want to get on with it. When they're in the elevator and they've punched their buttons, they want the doors to close and the box to move so they can be spit out on some other floor where their doctors or dentists or lawyers await them.

Victor has the grace, at least, to hurry the last few steps and thank the gray-haired lady for holding the door. "Twelve...Oh, it's already lit. Going to twelve?" he asks jovially, inappropriately. What the hell business of it is his where the little old lady's going?

"Oh, no," she says as if his question is a gracious, polite, well-bred one. "I get off at five. The American Lady Gym" she says. "I work out every day. I do think it's so important to stay in shape, don't you?"

"Absolutely," he responds. "Good for you!"

The woman beams, affirmed.

That's when he finally looks over to the other body in the
elevator. The one pressed in the far corner, watching through
narrowed eyes, without a trace of a smile on her lips.

"Claire!"

"Hello, Victor."

"I didn't even see you."

"I know."

"Going to twelve?"

"Yes, of course. Where else?"

The little lady gets off at five.

"Enjoy your workout," Victor tells her.

"Oh, I will," she replies. "I always do."

"By the way——" Victor clears his throat as the elevator
doors close, leaving them alone together in this tiny box. It's a
nervous habit he has and it drives her crazy. "I'd like to switch
this weekend for next so I can take Sean and Jennie to the
ball game. Margie's mom works for the Mariners and she got
us free tickets."

Victor. What a perfect name. Victor. A man who always
has to have his way. "I've already got plans for this week-
end," Claire lies, hoping it doesn't show, though it usually
does. Victor could always spot an insincerity. But Jesus, this
is what, only about the sixteenth time in the two years they've
been separated that he's pulled this?

He looks surprised though, instead of suspicious. The key
to spotting an insincerity, Victor always bragged, is not to be
emotionally involved in the consequences of the insincerity.
The sequelae, as he and his stuffy friends would put it. "Oh?"
He keeps it to one slightly started syllable. So she knows that
he's involved in the consequences. It pleases her. Ever since she
moved out, he's been keeping an eye on her social life. Gloating,
it has seemed to her, that she doesn't really have any.

Claire looks up at the floor indicator. "We're not going any-where," she notes.

"I thought you just said you had plans."

"No, I mean we're not going anywhere. You and I."

"I disagree. We've gotten a lot of stuff figured out. But you know what they say about the devil being in the details."

"No. We are not moving in this elevator. We have been between nine and ten for the past couple of minutes and there's no movement in the elevator."

He stares at her blankly.

She hates this about him. He can be so oblivious to the utterly obvious. Like the time she had to explain to him that the policeman who stopped them was giving them a ticket. Like the time Sean was screaming his head off in pain when he fell out of the maple tree and Victor asked "Does it hurt?" Like asking her if she's going to twelve. Is it symbolic, she won-ders, that they've been married for twelve years, and now their attorneys await them on the twelfth floor?

"The elevator is stuck." She says it slowly, distinctly, a ser-rated edge in her voice.

He hates that about her. That way she has of talking to him like he's an idiot. If he's such an idiot, how come he has a Ph.D. from Harvard? They don't give doctorates to idiots, not the last time he checked. Not at Harvard, anyway. Maybe at that diploma mill where she got her so-called Masters. But not where he comes from. Claire. What an irony, he thinks. A name that means clear, but she's so damn muddle-brained she can't see the real picture.

"Stuck" he says.

"Maybe we should press the emergency call button."

"Maybe we should. It's only been a couple of minutes though. No need to panic."

"I'm not panicked. But I have no desire to be late to this meeting. You know both of these guys are going to charge us whether we're on time or not."

"I suppose you could have picked a cheaper attorney."

"Victor, don't start on that. You could have, too."

"So should I hit this button?"

"I say hit it."

The raucous buzzing jangling shrieking bell could be an amplification of some cellular nerve ending sort of thing. Some audio translation of the tension in the space.

He looks up at the ceiling in exasperation. There they are, top down. There's a mirror up there. He is suddenly aware that it reveals to her how much more hair he's lost since she last kissed that spot.

There is no response to the alarm button.

"What does that say?"

"What?"

"That panel."

"Where?"

"That one right there. By the buzzer."

"Can't you read it?"

"I forgot my glasses." She hates to admit this. She hates having to wear glasses to see small print and she hates acknowledging her dependence on them.

"It says 'in case of emergency'—that's this I'd say—'open door and lift phone.'" He opens the little door and lifts the receiver that is tucked inside. "What should I tell them?"

"That we're stuck!" Jesus, she thinks. How can someone who is so educated be so incredibly inept, so dysfunctional in such elementary circumstances.

"Hello? Yes. Yes. Looks like ten. Yes, I see. Oh, my!...Oh my! Yes, uh hum, yes, I believe I can."

"What?" she demands. One of those irritating habits. She gets scared, then she interrupts, then she apologizes. Then she interrupts again. "I'm sorry. What?" she repeats.

He shakes his head at her, puts his fingers to his lips in a shushing gesture.

"Fuck you," she silently mouths to him.

"Thank you," he says aloud to the person on the other end of the receiver. He hangs up. "We're stuck," he says.

"No duh," she says.

"All the elevators are out. The whole building is out. A computer glitch of some kind."

"How soon will they fix it?"

"I don't know. First they have to figure out what's causing it."

"Don't they have a back-up system or something?"

"I didn't ask."

"Call them back and ask."

"I don't think I should bother them."

"Bother them?"

"Look, they're trying to figure it out. I don't think we should interrupt them." Sometimes he thinks basic common sense is something that just passed her by.

"I'm sure the person who answers the phone isn't part of whoever's trying to figure it out."

"He said 'we.'"

"Huh?"

"He said 'We're trying to figure it out.' He didn't say 'They're trying to figure it out.'"

This is when the lights go out. Claire fails to suppress a scream. She hates darkness. She always sleeps with the light on.

"Take it easy," he says.

"Why isn't there an emergency light?" she wants to know. "There should be a battery back-up."

"I don't know. Maybe the battery is dead."

Victor hates darkness too. He's never told her how much, because he was always the one who comforted her or the kids when they were afraid. He's remembering the time when Jenny was little: her third birthday, in fact, when Hurricane Dave took out the lights. Jenny was scared out of her wits, and Claire was no help at all. She yelled "Somebody get the candles!" and started to cry. Jenny picked right up on it and began to wail, amazingly like the wail of the fire engines when they started out of the station two blocks away from their— or what used to be their—house. She'd start low and slide up the scale like "Rhapsody in Blue," then when she hit the top she'd alternate between two shrieking notes. He wondered, if they'd lived next to an old-fashioned firehouse with a clanging bell, would Jenny have learned to clang when she was afraid instead of wail?

He can hear Claire breathing. Short terrified breaths. He knows she is shaking. He doesn't need a light on to know that. He's held that shaking person tightly in his arms more than once.

Today, he takes the approach he took with Jenny eight years ago.

"Claire?"

"What?" Her breathing makes her voice raspy.

"Got any birthday candles?"

Claire's labored breath splutters just a bit. He hopes it's a little giggle in spite of her fear.

It is. "Not with me."

"Got a lighter?"

"I stopped smoking."

"You did? Good for you!"

"I sure could use a cigarette right about now, though."

"Actually, I may have some matches, but we don't have any birthday candles to light anyway. Here we go, I've got three matches."

"Strike anywhere?"

"No, just book matches."

"What do you have matches for?"

"For the joint I also have. Want to share it?"

"Victor!"

"What?"

"You can't smoke marijuana in a public elevator."

"Who's going to know?"

"Get serious. They're going to rescue us any minute. Everybody knows what pot smells like. Besides, you know I haven't smoked since Jenny was conceived."

"Pot."

"What?"

"You haven't smoked pot since Jenny was conceived."

"What are you implying?"

This is a point of contention between them and Claire is not on unimpeachable ground. Her attorney has even told her about a case where a mom who wouldn't stop smoking lost primary custody of her son who had asthma to the boy's father, even though the dad was an unemployed alcoholic. Claire stopped smoking cigarettes two months ago, on the lawyer's advice. You never know who you're going to get on the bench, the attorney pointed out. The judge in this cautionary tale was an alcoholic himself, and a smug ex-smoker of some twenty years.

"Nothing, Claire. It was just a point of claire-ification, no pun intended."

"What pun?"

"Never mind."

There is a brief moment of silence but neither of them can stand it so they both start to speak at once. A few seconds of false starts like that and finally Victor says, "We could go over the terms. Make sure we agree. So that when we get out of here we'll have something to show for the time we spent. Like you say, we're probably going to get billed for the time anyway."

"Did I say that? It sounds like something you'd say."

"Me? I thought you said it."

"It's true, no matter who said it. Okay. What about holidays? Why are you insisting on every other Christmas when you're not even Christian?"

"Because that's when they get time off from school."

If Claire could think of a parry she would, but she is distracted by a wave of panic.

"Victor, would you sit where I can feel you? Just, you know, so I know you're there?"

"I'm here, Claire." Victor is distracted himself. He hates to see her suffer and though he can't technically see her suffer he can hear it in her voice. He gropes his way around the perimeter of the elevator until he's near her. God! She smells the same. He notes with alarm that an erection, unbidden, is asserting itself, accompanied by disconcertingly vivid images of having wild sex with Claire right there on the elevator floor. I used to love this woman, he thinks. What happened?

"Victor?"

"I'm right here." He stops as soon as he can feel her just a foot or so away.

"Victor?"

"What?"

"Can we call that guy again? See how it's going?"

"Of course we can. Why don't you call this time?"

"No, you. I'm too...I...I don't want them to hear how scared I am."

"How scared are you?"

"I'm very fucking scared. Victor, what if this is it?"

"What?"

"You know. IT. Maybe today is the day the earth's crust shifted or someone finally dropped the bomb. What if civilization as we know it has just *ended*."

"Claire, get a grip. The elevator's stuck. It's not the end of the world."

His tone of voice is suddenly reminding her of a decade of marriage. "Give me the phone."

Her tone of voice is suddenly reminding him of a decade of marriage. "It's over there," he says, "by the buttons."

"Light one of your matches so I can see," she says.

"Can't you just feel your way?"

"Oh, Jesus, Victor, just do it, will you? Why do you have to be so controlling?"

"Me controlling? Who's giving orders here?"

"Just do it."

"Who are you going out with this week-end, Phil Knight?"

"What are you talking about? Who's Phil Knight?"

"Never mind." He considers whether she's so ignorant of business and current affairs and corporate slogans that she really doesn't know who Phil Knight is and what "just do it" means.

There's the sound of rooting in the utter darkness of this box they occupy together. Victor listens for a moment, then has to ask "What the hell are you doing?"

"I'm looking for something in my purse."

"In the dark?"

"Well, obviously. Since you won't light your precious match. Here it is. Now. Will you please light just one match?"

"What you got?"

"An ear candle."

"A what?"

"An ear candle. It's something I bought to try cleaning my ears out. It should burn a lot longer than a match."

"An ear candle."

"Victor, will you stop repeating me. It drives me crazy."

"An ear candle," he repeats. "Don't hit me or I'll eat the matches."

She laughs in spite of herself. "Victor, intuit my lips. Light a match."

He does. She's holding a waxy tube.

"Now light this. Let's see how it works."

He holds the match to the end of the tube and they both watch the ear candle catch fire and begin to burn.

"How is this thing supposed to clean your ears?"

"You put the little end in your ear and as the other end burns it pulls your ear wax up the tube."

"Yeah, right."

"Well, you asked."

"And I was answered. Call the guy."

She looks at him through the flickering light. Twelve years I've been married to this condescending sonofabitch. This smug, judgmental know-it-all. Twelve years. More than a decade. More than a tenth of a century.

He looks at her through the flickering light. Twelve years I've been married to this dingbat. This master of muddle. Twelve years of putting up with every health care fad and fraud in sight. But damn! She still turns me on. "Call him."

She makes her way across the elevator. He fails to will his erection away, shifts his posture so that it will at least be less obvious, just in case the lights should come back.

Claire lifts the small receiver from its cradle. "Do I have to dial anything?"

"No," he says. "They pick it up automa—"

He is interrupted by her speaking to the man at the other end of the phone.

"Yes," Claire is saying, "yes, we had just passed the ninth floor when it stopped, and then a couple of minutes later, after my—" she stops herself from saying "my husband." They are, after all, on their way to attempt to settle their differences sufficiently to finalize their divorce. So she can't say my ex-husband either. "—After my about-to-be-ex-husband called, the lights went out, too. Oh, you know? Oh. Oh, I see."

Victor's erection is subsiding now of its own accord. His attention has shifted to following the conversation, trying to guess the other end of it. He's also trying to figure out how he likes being referred to as an about-to-be-ex-husband.

"What'd he say?" He wishes he could resist asking.

Her answer is drowned by the sound of the smoke alarm, triggered by the spirals of gray that curl off the end of the ear candle. She drops the flaming tube, slams her foot onto it, plunging them once again in darkness. "What?" she is shouting into the phone. "An ear candle.....AN EAR CANDLE....a candle, okay? Something we lit so we could see. It's out now. How do we get this thing to stop? I said HOW DO WE GET THIS THING TO STOP?"

Next to her, Victor is yelling, too. "TELL THEM TO TURN THE DAMN ALARM OFF!"

"SHUT UP, VICTOR, I'M TRYING TO HEAR HOW TO DO THAT! Okay, okay, I think I got it," she says now, into the phone, while she gropes the floor number panel in front of her and feels her way up two buttons from the bottom. "Okay, I got it. Okay." Mercifully, the alarm stops wailing.

Claire laughs. This confuses Victor. What happened to her fear of the dark?

"What's so funny?" he asks.

She ignores him and speaks into the phone. "Really! Like two weeks in Philadelphia!" She laughs again, falls silent for a moment.

This annoys Victor. He has always hated being the outsider in the presence of an in-joke. She knows this. She's doing this on purpose.

She guffaws. "You got that right!" she says, which annoys him doubly. Not only has he no idea what is amusing her, he hates that phrase. Every time she uses it, it irritates him. When did it start? She didn't say it when they first met. Surely he would have noticed. No, it started sometime after they were married, four or five years maybe. One day she said it for the first time and ever since she's been saying it and ever since it's been annoying the bejeezus out of him.

He told her once, back then, that it sounded ignorant.

"To whom?" she had said, emphasizing the "m" because he was a snob about using the correct form.

"To anyone with a sense of class," he'd said. "It makes you sound like trailer trash." Then of course he regretted his words. Claire had lived in a trailer park when she was a child, and her grandparents still lived in one. Damn, he'd thought to himself. I shouldn't have said that, she'll just be defensive now.

Claire had narrowed her eyes to angry slits. "You got that right" she'd spit at him before propelling herself briskly, furiously, out of the room.

Now she laughs again, aware of his displeasure and exulting in it. "Okay," she says into the phone. "Uh hum. Okay. Sure." She laughs again, a smug, throaty laugh. She knows it's a smug laugh, so does he. "Thanks. Yes, I'm sure...yes....Good-bye."

"What in blazes was that all about?"

She smiles in the dark.

"Well? What did he say?" Victor is frustrated, aware that he sounds like he cares too much.

"That they've got a crew working on it."

"No shit."

"Victor, that phrase. It makes you sound so middle school, you know what I mean?"

She's sassy. That's what he had fallen for when he first met her. He knew he tended to be pompous, and she was one of the few women he'd met who could take him down a peg. Of the other two, one was his mother and the other was the dancer he'd dated for a time, until she broke her ankle and started to put on weight. Victor liked her, but he just couldn't get excited about a woman who didn't have the self-control to keep in shape. Claire keeps in shape. And she's witty. She wasn't afraid of him then. And she apparently isn't afraid of him now. Of the dark, but not of him.

He isn't really middle school, she thinks. He is...exotic, almost, his middle-school expressions aside. Classy. He knows which wines go with which main courses. He'd even have the nerve and knowledge to send a bottle back at a restaurant if he didn't think it was up to standards. She would never be able to do that. And when she teased him about his pretensions he delighted in it, told her no other woman had the wit, the intelligence, the nerve to talk to him like that. She closes her eyes in the pitch dark cubicle and smiles at her memories. And he is a good father. When things went to hell between them he didn't bail on the visits and child support the way some do.

"What are you thinking?" His voice intrudes, reminds her that she dislikes telling him what she is thinking. She used to love confiding in him. Till he started using her confidences against her. He doesn't seem to have realized that was then, this is now. She is silent.

Victor is not a man who can stand much silence. He fills it quickly. "I'm thinking maybe we could go over our list, see if we can come to some agreements while we wait. What you want to bet Sharksky and Butch will charge us for the time we're stuck in here anyway."

"I don't like homophobic jokes."

"Come on, she's butch. She's got that short short hair they all have. She's pushy like a man. What can I say?"

"You could say nothing."

"You got a crush on her or something?"

"Victor, stop it. She's my attorney and her sexual preferences are nobody's business but her own."

"I'm sorry, it's just that..."

"Victor!"

"All right! So can we talk?"

She sighs. "We can try."

"All right then. I want the kids at Christmas on alternate years."

"What am I supposed to do?"

"What do you mean?"

"I don't want to be alone on Christmas."

"Hey, guess what? Neither do I."

"But your family...."

"Isn't Christian. Good lord, Claire, what is this, the Spanish Inquisition?"

"I just mean it's not an emotional family time for you."

"Oh? Number one: it's very emotional to have the entire world around you act like Christmas is everyone's holiday whether it is or not. Number two: what's so special about your family's tradition of overcooked turkey and stewed uncles?

You never go to church. You're not a Christian either. You're a goddamn Buddhist. Isn't that what you told me?"

"It's not a religious thing. It's cultural."

"Claire, we're talking about basic fairness here. Cut the crap."

Silence. Claire admits to herself that she's been talking crap. Out loud: "Okay. I get them this year."

"Fine."

"What's next?"

"I went first. How 'bout you bring up something from your list."

"A college fund."

"What?"

"I want you to make regular contributions to a college fund."

"Look, they'll do better keeping their grades up and getting good scholarships. It was how we both did it."

"And if they don't keep a 4.0?"

"They have to. You have to have impeccable records."

"Reality check, Victor. Jenny is not like you and me. She works hard for a B+."

"I don't have a lot of extra cash lying around, Claire. This divorce has cost me plenty already."

"And it's almost over, isn't it? So your cash flow is going to improve. $400 a month. $200 each until they're out of college..."

Victor has to admit to himself that she's got a point. But come to think of it, Jenny might not even go to college.

"And what if..."

"...or twenty three, whichever comes first."

"You've got it all thought out, don't you?"

"I've had time." She is appalled to hear her voice catch.

"Oh?"

Damn it, she thinks. Don't cry now. Don't.

"You're the one who wanted out."

"Yes. I was." Don't. Don't give him that satisfaction.

"And you still want out?"

"Victor, I AM out. It doesn't matter whether I want it or not."

"I wish I could see you."

"Huh?"

"It's weird talking to you in the dark. I don't like not being able to see you. That's a big part of communication."

"Just think of it like voice e-mail."

"Claire, can I have some parentheses."

"What?"

"You know, the emoticon stuff."

"I'm not...I don't know what you're getting at."

"I'm asking for a hug."

 Silence.

"Parentheses?"

"Don't you ever send anyone an on-line hug?"

"No."

"You show it by putting their name inside a few sets of parentheses."

"Oh."

"I guess that means no?"

Something in his voice makes her want to rush to him and cradle him, stroke his hair, tell him everything is going to be all right. He sounds just like Sean when he saw a monster in his closet one night. She turned on the light for him to prove it was his nerf ball hoop with the ball balanced atop. Then said See? It's all right honey. You can go back to sleep. As she turned to leave, she heard that voice. Mom? Can I have a hug good night? It broke her heart. Of course he could! And then she got the nerf ball and said Tell you what. I'll take this monster's head with me and put it in my closet. That way, if he sees me, he won't have any legs to walk on. If his body wants to talk, he won't be able to see which way to go. We'll divide and conquer. She hugged him fiercely. Mom? Yes honey? What does conquer mean?

Now, here, in the dark, she is thinking why Victor? Why are you asking me for a hug?

Now, here, in the dark, Victor is wondering why? Why did I do that?

A moment of silence. He sits with his back against the wall of the elevator, the top of his head barely clearing the brass handrail just above it. He hears tiny noises, brushing, whishing sounds of movement across the carpeted floor and then the electric touch of her hand. It hits his upper arm first, as she waves through the air to locate his body. From there it travels down to his elbow, forearm, wrist, and comes to rest by lacing its fingers into his own.

"Victor," she says. He has never before heard such heaviness in her voice. Such weariness. Has it never been there before, or has he never listened to it before?

"I'm sorry," she continues, "that it didn't work out. I'm so sorry. I did love you once."

He pulls her to him and embraces her, comforting this woman who left him, this mother of his children, this enigma. What else had she wanted? He'd always thought theirs was an ideal marriage. He almost asks if she wants to try again. At this moment, there is no conscious memory for him of another woman, who will be waiting to hear the story of this adventure. It is only his fear that she will laugh that prevents him from voicing it. He murmurs her name and leaves it at that.

The Muzak comes on first. It has moved, apparently played on during their wait. "Pennies from Heaven" has given way to "Dancing in the Dark."

She pulls into herself. He lets her go. They never did dance together, really. It was Margie who got him to take up ballroom and popular dancing, so that now it's part of their routine. He starts to stand, hits his head on the brass rail, and suppresses a curse. He doesn't want to sound out of control.

She grabs the rail and hauls herself up. She doesn't want to be sitting on the floor like a little kid or something.

The lights return, a flicker, another, and then they creak on the way fluorescents do.

Claire and Victor exchange an uncomfortable, embarrassed glance, and move away from each other. The elevator lurches ever so slightly and there are whirring sounds somewhere in the distance, coming, perhaps, from the bottom of the shaft.

Claire crosses the cubicle to get her purse. Victor kicks his left leg out to banish the kink in his knee.

"What time is it?" Claire asks.

"Two-thirty."

"Shall we see if they're still waiting for us?"

"Sure, why not?"

She pushes the button for twelve and they continue in their slow ascent.

Fencing

JOAN GIVES ME the look. She stirs her tea: red tea, because
she's a fan of that Botswana detective, the fat fictional one
who always drinks red bush tea. She stirs her tea, clanking
the spoon, then lifting it from the cup and thrusting it at me,
punctuating her stare.

"What?" I ask.

"You need to talk to him."

"Why? What will that accomplish?" We're talking about a
guy, our neighbor over the back fence, who tosses wine bottles into our yard at the rate of four or five a week. She's been
in a bind about how to respond. I have proposed getting a
motion-activated flood light system installed so the next time
a wine bottle flies over the fence it gets lit up like Kliegs are on
it. "Like the president says," I say, "light is the best disinfectant."

"He said sunlight," Joan says. "Not any light. Not flood
lights at night. Sunlight."

"The principle is the same. When you have something
shady going on, you take a look at it in bright light."

"Natural bright light."

"Yeah, well, he's not tossing them in natural light, is he?"

"Why don't you just go talk to him? Tell him if he's the one
throwing bottles into our yard, to please stop. And if it's not
him, then..."

"If?" I counter.

"Well, it could be someone else."

"Like who?"

"Maybe someone comes in our yard at night to drink."

"Not likely."

"But not impossible," she parries.

My wife should have been a trial lawyer. She likes to argue. Instead she's a therapist. I'm a CPA. I prefer to deal with numbers. Numbers don't lie. They either add up or they don't.

"Are you afraid to talk to him?"

"I just don't see what good it would do."

"I think you're afraid to talk." She sips her tea, then purses her lips and raises her eyebrows as if she's proved something. "I think you're afraid to confront him. Because it might not be him, and then you'd have to rethink your theory."

"Stop analyzing me. Why don't *you* talk to him? Since you have clearly thought out exactly what to say to have exactly the effect you would like to have."

"What's that supposed to mean?"

"Nothing. It doesn't mean anything."

That's the end of that conversation. Joan makes herself busy rinsing the wine bottles out to put them into recycling. She insists. I tell her it's ridiculous to rinse them. She reads to me from the instructions that come with our solid waste bill: "Clean glass bottles and jars, no caps or lids."

Our neighbor almost always leaves the caps on. Which tells you something about the kind of wine he drinks.

Anyway, I deliberately disengage and the whole conversation dissipates as it always does until two weeks later. It's recycling time, and we have another twelve bottles to make presentable for the recyclers.

"I think," she announces at breakfast, "something else could be at work here. It could be a passive-aggressive response to the blackberries along the back fence. Maybe the expression of someone who is afraid to say directly, 'Cut those damn blackberries.' I'd do it myself, but I threw my shoulder out."

"There will be no cutting blackberries until the fruit has ripened and we've made jam."

"We could make less jam," she says. "We never use up all the jam we make anyway. Or we could move them to another part of the yard."

"You don't move blackberries. They move you." A clever riposte if I do say so myself.

"Very funny."

"Seriously, if you want blackberries in some other part of the yard all I have to do is stop mowing it there for, oh, four or five hours."

She's giving me the look so I just restate my position. We are neither cutting nor moving blackberries. We will cut blackberries after we've made jam. It is not logical to waste resources.

The bottles keep coming. Thirteen during the two weeks the blackberries ripened. I rinse them out. She burned her finger making jam and doesn't want to get the bandage wet.

She's watching me pour out the remnants of a bottle. "It's a shame to waste wine. You know what I think? Could be a secret alcoholic. That's why sometimes there's wine left in the bottles. Someone comes home, interrupts the drinking, so out goes a partially-consumed bottle before the drinking is discovered. So sad." Over empathizing is an occupational hazard for her.

"Most of the time the bottles are empty," I point out.

"Which proves my point," she says. "Think about it."

She looks like she's about to cry, so I don't argue.

I do an online search for motion detection systems but I don't tell her. I don't want to get into another argument.

"The bottle numbers are going up," she says. "It's not good to drink alone."

"He probably had a friend over and that's why there are

more bottles this time. There are two that aren't the usual labels. Somebody brought them over and they sat in the back yard, polished 'em off together, then lobbed 'em over the fence."

"Let's see," she says.

"See what?"

"The ones that are different."

"They're already in the bin."

She goes dumpster diving to take a look.

"Just a different label," she says. "Still Chardonnay and Cabernet. But there's a price difference."

"What kind of difference?"

"Cheaper. It's usually the ten dollar stuff. These were six."

The jam-making season over, I cut the berries back. This reveals almost two dozen new bottles, under the brambles. Some clearly from the past, but four of them the newer, cheaper labels.

"I'm worried about this," she says on our next recycling day.

"Because he's drinking cheaper stuff?"

"Exactly. I wonder if there are economic pressures. If there's a job-related factor."

"What job?"

"Whatever. Could be self-employed and just not making enough. Maybe afraid to discuss it with anyone."

"Just worry about your own business," I say. "Keep your therapeutic nose out of his."

Yet another two weeks go by. Joan has taken to patrolling the back fence on a daily basis, to get a precise count of bottles per week and an accurate read on which days our neighbor drinks the most. Turns out he's one a day the first week, then goes to two. Furthermore, he alternates red and white.

"That is weird," I tell her.

"OCD," she diagnoses. "This is a person who feels compelled

to do things in very particular ways. Like drinking red wine one day and white the next. I wonder if it's the same with the rest of the diet."

"Meaning?"

"Meaning maybe fish or chicken one night, beef or lamb the next."

"Maybe he's a vegetarian," I say.

"Whatever it is, it's escalating. This is a person in trouble, falling apart, wanting someone to notice. And no one—*no one*—is paying any attention."

"Flat out ridiculous. The bottom line is you're reading too much into this."

"You live in your head too much," she counters. "Not enough in your feelings."

"Whoa," I say. "I live in my head because it's trustworthy. Rationality is very comforting. You should try it sometime."

"It's not disconnected." She's on the verge of tears. "You may think you're in your head and that it's all logical and rational, but your brain is just part of your body. At times, an astonishingly small part."

I employ an indirect approach, distracting her with a tease. "Yes, Dr. Freud!" I know it pisses her off when I call her that. Particularly because I know full well she is not a Freudian. It works. She's mad now instead of tearful.

"Like right now," she says. "You think you're being witty and cerebral, but you're really being an ass."

The next night she serves wine with dinner. Cheap red wine. This is not common. Usually she drinks that red tea shit. She's determined to make me engage. I'm determined not to comment on it. She pours us each a glass. She's made lamb shank for dinner, with brown rice and carrots. It goes like this:

"How's the lamb?"

"Delicious, as always," I say. "Very tender. And the presentation is elegant."

Silence.

"The carrots okay? Not overcooked?"

"Not in the least. Perfect. Just a bit of crunch."

"The rice is a little gummy."

"It's hard to get rice right."

"The wine's not too bad, for a screw cap."

"Mmmmm."

"You don't like it?"

"It's okay. Marginal at best." I sip it slowly. She downs hers and pours another. Pours more in my glass, too. "Do we have to finish the bottle tonight?"

"No, of course not."

The next night it's halibut with Chardonnay. Cheap Chardonnay. "Is there any of that red left?" I ask.

"I tossed it," she says.

"Too bad. It was better than this crap, at least."

She gives me the look.

"I think," she says, "you should talk to the guy. Since you're so convinced it's him. Maybe that'll be the end of it. Or maybe..."

"You really should quit trying to get into everyone else's head all the time."

"And you should try it sometime," she flicks a piece of rice from her plate, aiming for me. "Seems kind of like you're afraid of real communication. Afraid of actual engagement. You'd rather install motion detector lights."

I assure her I've decided against that idea. It's true enough. I've settled on a different plan.

I take the next Monday off work and install a home security camera I bought on sale over the weekend. It's easy enough to conceal it in the Gravenstein and run the power cord from the monitor in the garage through the blackberries. I paid more than I wanted for it, but there's a nice little feature. It'll email me if anything unusual shows up on the tape. While I'm down there, I pick up the accumulated bottles for the week thus far: one red, one white. All the same six dollar crap Joan thinks it's funny to serve with dinner now. I'm planning to tell her about the security camera, but the thought flees my mind when she gets home. She's not alone. She's got the guy with her.

"I ran into Wiley on my way home from the bus stop and invited him to dinner."

"Hi," he says, pumping my hand. "Long time, no see." Our nefarious neighbor over the back fence.

"I ordered a pizza for supper," Joan says. "I hope you don't mind. I just don't feel like cooking tonight. I called from work and put in for a 6:30 delivery, so they should be here any minute."

"Can I get you something to drink?" I ask Wiley. "Beer? Wine? Red bush tea?"

"Water's fine," Wiley says.

Joan looks at me significantly, like I'm supposed to know what she wants. Finally, she says, "I'll take red. Wine."

"I thought you threw it out."

"There's another bottle in the pantry. Next to the vinegar and oil."

"Good thing it's labeled clearly. I could easily get confused: cheap wine, vinegar, vinegar, cheap wine…"

"Don't press it," Joan warns.

Wiley is looking at the books on our book shelves, avoiding our in-fighting. "Feldman and Hammer," he exclaims. "Boy, that takes me back."

"To what?" Joan wants to know.

"I had this book as a text in college," he says. *The Myth of Communication*. Very provocative, as I recall."

"It really changed the way I think about mental health," Joan says.

The doorbell rings. The delivery guy delivers. I go get the wine and water. Joan sets the table. We sit down to eat sausage, mushroom, extra cheese pizza.

"I hope you're not a vegetarian." Joan is suddenly apologetic. Sausage is for me, mushroom is for her, extra cheese we both like. I guess she didn't ask him what he wanted.

"Not to worry," Wiley says. "I'll eat anything." He laughs like he's just told a joke. Joan makes a point of laughing with him.

"Sure you don't want any wine, pal?" I pour myself a large glass and pass the bottle to Joan.

"Nope," he says. "I can't drink wine. Never could. Gives me a headache. Allergic to sulfites." He takes the piece of pizza I had my eye on: the one with the most sausage on it. Sonofabitch.

"Allergic, huh? That's a shame." What a dickwad. Pretending innocence. I look over to catch Joan's eye, but she's rearranging mushrooms into patterns on her pizza.

The next day it's nine o'clock before I can get away from work. I check my email before I leave for the house. There's something on the tape. By the time I get home, Joan is already in bed. There's a note about a headache and leftover pizza for supper. I head out to the garage.

The figure on the film isn't clear at first. It's not Wiley. As the culprit steps further into the frame, the image resolves: a woman about 5'4", wearing my wife's rain jacket and hat. She pulls a bottle out from under the jacket and places it on the ground. Huh. Joan all along? So this is some elaborate practical joke? I'm beginning to get it. This is her idea of some kind of game. "Touché," I whisper to myself. I smile. I'll think of something simple, yet unexpected for my counter move. But then she does something I don't understand at all. She sits down, right there next to the blackberries, and even without sound on the tape it's obvious. She's sobbing.

Half-Full

MA IS ALWAYS a half-full kind of gal, as she herself has always said. Not glass half-full optimist, but half full of it. In her youth, she cherished dreams of soloing big time, à la Lily Tomlin. She did standup comedy until some dude stood her up and left her in the lurch. "This is what a lurch looks like," she used to tell me, sweeping her arm to indicate the tiny Upper West Side walk-up that I have called home ever since I was old enough to say the word.

Ma was in her thirties then. Now she's on her deathbed in Beth Israel. She's come to specialize in geriatric jokes. "Esther ran into Mary the other day," she tells me. "Peered at her a good long time. You know her memory's not so good anymore. Then confessed, 'help me to remember,' she said, 'was it you or your sister who died last year?'"

I smile, because if I don't, Ma will furrow her wracked brow, say "Whazzamatter, still don't know a joke when you hear one?" and commence to cough, which I cannot stand. It sounds like her bones are breaking to tiny bits that will be ejected along with the ghastly green effluvia and bloody red clots that come up and bloom into the ghost white tissue she valiantly holds to her mouth. Ma has always prided herself on being a role model. She always covers her cough.

"Oh, and did you hear about old George Tompkins?" she goes on. "Finally kicked the bucket at 135." She pauses.

I know my cue. "Yeah?"

"Died of shock when he heard his grandfather was dating his ex-wife."

When I was growing up Ma would practice on me, always looking for the day she'd get a chance to audition again. If I had friends over, she'd corner them and do her whole routine, starting with the guy who tells his friend to meet him at the corner of Wait and Walk, ending with the one about pessimist and optimist boys: one is presented with a pony and can think only of the inevitable and distasteful stall cleaning that will be necessary while his happy brother, placed in a room full of poop, is convinced that a pony has to be nearby. "Your mom's a million laughs," they'd tell me, and they'd never come back.

As I grew older and less responsive she decided I was a hopeless sidekick and installed a series of dogs in the household to replace me as straight man. She named them after the theaters she dreamed of playing in: Biltmore, Plymouth, Helen Hayes, Shubert. She taught each of them to sit attentively when she told a joke and bark happily at the punch line. Shubert is the current shill-in-residence. He's a Jack Russell-poodle mix the pet store called a terri-poo but mom calls a Perrier. Shubert, she likes to say, is a cockeyed optimist, unlike me. They don't let dogs in the hospital so she's had to make do with a pessimist as her captive audience again.

She's on a roll now. "Three older friends, we'll call them senior citizens, are shooting the breeze and talking about what ails them. 'My memory is really going,' says the first. 'I find myself standing in front of my refrigerator with the door open and I can't remember if I'm hungry and looking for something to eat or if I've just finished putting away leftovers.'

'I know exactly what you mean,' says the second, 'I'll stop to rest on the stair landing and forget whether I was going up or down.'

"'I'm very lucky,' says the third. 'My memory is as sharp as ever, knock on wood.'" Ma punctuates this with three sharp taps of her knuckles on the hospital tray. "'Oh, there's someone at the door! I'd better get it.'"

Behind me, I hear laughter and turn to see the nurse in the doorway. "Time to check your vitals," she chirps.

As she bends to place fingers on Ma's pulse and time her heartbeat, a tear rolls down her cheek. Recovering her composure she says, "Your mother slays me. She just kills me. She should be on Broadway."

I tell Ma goodbye, that it's time for her to get some rest and for me to walk Shubert, but she hardly notices. She's found a warmer house to play to. "I ever tell you the one about the young wife who was making a ham for dinner?"

Shubert greets me at the door with the exuberant hope and joy that is the trademark of small dogs with small brains. He knows, like the boy in the room full of shit knows. He just knows. There's got to be a pony around here somewhere.

Turn, Turn, Turn

HE SHUFFLES OH so carefully, with a little hitch and a little swing to get each foot forward when it is time for it to go forward. It's the system Robert Thompson has devised to keep himself from falling. Holding his hand against the pale blue wallpaper, paper he pasted there when Eisenhower was president and no one had ever walked on the moon, he works his way into the front room of the house. Past the framed photograph of a scrubbed cherubic girlchild, her black braids reflecting bright sunlight, her infectious smile missing two front teeth. Past the "Footprints" prayer, carefully laminated and trimmed. Past the wall calendar, annotated with birthdays, anniversaries, due dates for bills and medication schedules. *That white woman is still there.* In his chair. Plaid shirt, blue jeans. *Dressed like she lives here.* She's reading a book. She glances up at him, she smiles. He turns, step-shuffles back to the hallway. Hand on wall, he traces his way to the bedroom door, then turns and stands there for some time, looking back into the room at her. She speaks. "If there's anything you need, Mr. Thompson, just let me know."

"Thank you." He's aware of the lilt in his voice, the emphasis that shows his appreciation is genuine. He just might need something. He just might. But where is that other woman who gets him what he needs? The one with chocolate brown skin and pepper gray hair. He's deeply puzzled by her absence. He turns away from the bedroom and carefully rounds the corner into the kitchen.

Now, for a moment, he forgets his dilemma. Something in

a bowl on the counter distracts him. *Looks like it might be good to eat.* It's right there, right in front of him. He takes some in his hand and tastes it. It's a familiar taste. *Macaroni.* His mind grabs the word. Ah, but then that woman peeks in from the other end of the kitchen. He knows suddenly that the food isn't supposed to be in his hand. He hurriedly puts it to his mouth and manages to stuff most of the macaroni in, hiding the evidence. He expects to be scolded: has a sudden picture of his mother flash through his memory. But this woman—the one who has appeared in his house, in his kitchen—her face tells him she feels as if she has intruded.

"Do you mind if I get myself a drink of water?" He mutely acknowledges her request, hitches to the side to let her pass to the sink. He watches while she finds a glass in the cupboard, fills it with cold water, drinks it down. Then he turns and makes his way into the hallway again.

He can hear her washing the glass out, placing it in the dish drainer. From his vantage point in the hallway, he sees her return to his chair in the living room and resume reading the book. The woman he's looking for reads out loud to him from this book. But she would never sit in his chair. She sits in one of the straight back chairs from the dining alcove. She reads something to him every night from this book. She reads of the abundance of blessing in the world. He considers asking the strange woman to read to him. *Did she say she would? I can't remember.*

He turns to collect his thoughts. There is a door in front of him. He opens the door. His thoughts are not there. He turns back toward the living room. "Now who are you?" he asks, finally admitting his confusion.

She smiles. The smile reminds him of someone, but he can't quite place who that would be. "I'm Deanna, your next door neighbor, Mr. Thompson. Your daughter Rosalie called to ask me to stay with you until she gets here. She went with Mrs. Thompson to the hospital, but she'll be here soon."

Robert Thompson frowns. These words "Rosalie," "Mrs. Thompson," "hospital:" they don't hold any particular meaning for him at this moment. Or perhaps they do. He's not sure. He turns, faces the bathroom door. He turns. He faces the bedroom door. He is looking for a woman with brown skin and gray hair. He turns again. There is another door. *Where did all these doors come from?* He opens it, revealing a steep descending staircase, with a gate across the top step. It frightens him, makes him fear he may fall. He closes that door and holds the wall. There is something else he is trying to remember. He focuses on his feet, hitches himself along and inches back into the kitchen again. This woman calls him Mr. Thompson. Most of them, most white women, call him Robert or even Bob. His mother called him Robert. Always. And when she was angry, she called him Robert Edward Thompson. She was tall, like him; thin too, like him. He hasn't seen her for a long time, except in his dreams. The woman he is looking for now is the one who can call him Bob, or even Baby, without offending him. *Where is she?* He opens the refrigerator. Not in there. He closes the refrigerator. It's the refrigerator they bought the day that plane blew up over Scotland. *That was on the news when we brought it in and...*there's something else he is trying to remember. There's a feeling in his bladder, a kind of pressure. *I ought to remember what to do about that.* He starts toward the dining alcove.

He stops when he sees that woman. She is reading the book. *Sitting in my chair. Anna—that's it, the name of the woman...my wife...she read to me about there being a time for everything. A time to sow, a time to die, and...something about stones.*

Anna would know what to do about this feeling. Anna isn't here. *This woman who is here is watching me.* "Are you hungry, Mr. Thompson?" asks the stranger. "Did you have supper yet?" Something like an old radio with bad reception sounds in his head. It says "Robert Edward Thompson." A warm feeling spreads, a wet feeling.

He feels a sudden need to dissemble. "I got rid of it already," he chuckles. The woman nods noncommittally, a weak, tentative smile on her face. Then she turns away, like she got caught doing something she shouldn't.

Oh, he misses Anna. Suddenly, it makes him want to cry. He notices the telephone and he remembers her talking about him. Not on the telephone, though. She was outside, in the back. *She was telling someone, telling that woman!—that woman sitting in my chair—telling her when she asked if I wanted my supper I said I'd rather wait till my wife got home.* "It doesn't do me a bit of good to worry about it," she had said. "I wait ten minutes and he knows who I am. That's just how he is. In and out, in and out. Mostly out, but every now and then he's just as clear as he can be. Then it goes away again. I told him, 'you sure must've known something like this would happen to be so good to me all those years.' That's the truth, too. Nobody had it better than I did. He was always here for me. Always here. And you know he did everything around the house. He put the roof on this house. He built that garage. He put these shingles on. Oh, he kept it up so well. I sure can't expect him to do any of that now, and you know I'm not about to get up on this ladder and fix anything. That's why I'm putting concrete down here. I don't want any more grass to mow." Robert had stepped through the door then, holding the telephone

receiver. "What you got there, Baby?" she'd asked. "Put it back,
Bob." Then she'd turned to the woman at the fence and chuckled. "I got to go on inside now. He's liable to try to cook that
telephone, or flush it down the toilet. He doesn't know what it
is anymore." And Anna had put down the concrete patio block
she'd been about to install, then turned to hurry up the steps.
She took the telephone and she said I was always here.

What would Anna say to him now? Would she scold him
about his wet pants? He thinks she might. *But she wouldn't
call me Robert Edward.* Would she help him change his
clothes? He knows she would. Would she ask what he needs?
He would like that. He could tell her he needs dry pants. He
can't tell this other woman. *Why, I hardly even know her.*

She is getting up and walking to the front window, walking away from Robert's restless shuffling and turning. She is
looking out the window. Now she is turning too, returning to
his chair. Robert has been facing that room from his post in
the hallway. He hurriedly turns away. *She knows. She knows
I'm wet....* "Can I help you with anything?" she asks and the
vagueness annoys him. They both know what she means. Why
does she have to beat around the bush?

"No!" He feels almost ferocious. *Well, that answered her.*
She's back to the book. She picks it up and sits down again.
This morning, or maybe it was some other morning, Anna
had read to him from that book. She'd read that all prayers are
answered. Robert tries to remember what a prayer is.

He turns his back to the woman. He looks at the toilet.
It makes him angry. Then again, he can't quite remember
what he is angry about. He turns back to the living room. He
hitches and shuffles into it. He looks behind a chair next to
the door against the wall. She's not there. Brown, big-boned
woman. Grey hair. *She calls me Baby, makes me milkshakes,*

holds me, helps me get my feet up on the bed when I'm tired and want to go to sleep. And all these doors! With nothing useful behind them! And I would like to lie down on the bed but I need that woman to help me and I'm not supposed to lie down on the bed because my clothes are wet. She has enough to do without having to change the sheets every day.

The thoughts leave as suddenly as they came. He is staring blankly at a stranger in his chair. The chair he's had since Kennedy was shot. He sat in that chair the day he watched the march. He doesn't remember that now. He doesn't remember anything right at this second. A dull panic washes up on him. He steadies himself, holds the wall. The panic recedes.

The woman in the chair jumps up now and crosses to the window. "They're here," she announces.

Next thing he knows, there's a whole bunch of people coming through the front door. One of them looks a little familiar. *Ms. Fancy, with her blue suit and pink blouse.* The other three he's never seen before. White coats, all of them. *They've got a damn bed in the middle of my living room.*

"Papa," says the one who reminds him of someone, "you're going to go somewhere where they can take care of you. Mama can't come home for at least a week, probably two. She's tired; she needs to rest. She can't take care of you until she comes home. These folks are going to take you to Sunset Acres. It's a place where they can take care of you."

Why does she have to repeat herself?

"Hi, Bob." There's a little thing with a skirt that's way too short. "Can I get you to sit down on the cot?"

"No, I don't believe so," he replies carefully, politely, in spite of her impertinence. "I believe I'll wait for my wife to come home."

"She's not coming home tonight, Papa," Ms. Fancy says, an

edge to her voice. *There's no need to be irritated.* "You need to go with these folks so you can get some sleep tonight."

"I'm not tired."

"Papa," says the woman, and surprises him by crying, "Papa, I can't stay here with you. And this lady has to go home too." She nods her head at the one who took his chair. He blinks slowly, and feels his hands move as if trying to grasp something.

One of the young men speaks now. The other listens and nods. "Bob, I'm going to help you sit down on the edge of the cot." Suddenly they surround him, force him off his feet. Fear of the fall takes him over. A little sob escapes. *Who are these people?* She wouldn't let them do this. If she were here. *Where is she?* Their hands are all over him, oh my god, even on his wet clothes and now he's sitting, belted to the cot, held in place by straps. He didn't even see those before. Where did they come from?

"We want to make sure you don't get up and run away on us," says the short skirt one, flashing him a smile like she just told a joke. It's not funny. Where in the world would he get up and run to? *Someone should talk some sense into her. It's not right to show that much skin to people.*

"Papa, I'll ride to the home with you." He can feel a terror rising up; it's like a flood from somewhere...somewhere he doesn't want to remember now. But he does suddenly remember the chair woman. *She helped me up once when I fell in the yard. She and my wife. Where is my wife?*

The one who pushed him first is talking again. "We want to help you, Bob. We don't want you to get hurt. But we can only help you if you help us. Cooperate with us. Rosalie says you've had a couple of falls. We don't want that to happen again. That's why we have to have the straps on. So you don't fall." The man glances at the others now, and Robert Thompson is not won by the smug look on his face. Robert has seen that look before, but he can't place where.

There is an urgent, heavy silence. The clock that has been on the mantle since Jackie Robinson played for the Brooklyn Dodgers is ticking.

"Bob, we're going to take you to Sunset Acres now."

Mr. Robert Thompson looks at the assembled faces. One he thinks he might know. One who's been sitting in his favorite chair all evening long, though he's been too polite to point it out to her. One in a disgraceful little skirt. The man who pushed him down. The one who helped him do it. White coats, short skirt, plaid shirt, pink blouse. All kinds of people. Men, women, white, brown. But she's not there.

They surround him, smiling, staring. One calls him Papa, one calls him Mr. Thompson, three call him Bob. But *she's not here*. The strong, warm woman who makes him milkshakes and calls him Baby and tells him where to hang up the phone and where to pee and helps him put his feet up when he is tired. *She is not here.*

"Bob, you're coming with us now, okay?" Then, in a moment like lightning, he knows exactly who these people are. He's been expecting them. He's been expecting them for some time. He's surprised it's taken them so long to get there. *Poor Anna. I've really worn her out. Of course she needs a rest.*

"Well," he says, looking steadily, solemnly around the circle. "I guess I don't have much choice now, do I?" He leans forward against the restraining straps. Instinctively, they all close in a bit.

Every one of them could stand a lesson in manners. "Get me my hat, please," adds Robert Thompson. "If you don't mind."

Answering

"WE'RE STILL HERE. Good." It was what Howard said to his heart every morning since the first day of the sudden unexplained pain.

A man of well-established routine peppered with very occasional impulse, Howard had decided to walk across the bridge that day from southwest to northwest Portland. His daughter Stephanie was performing in a little theater on Ratcliffe Street, and he'd promised her he'd come to see her. He rarely liked the plays she got roles in, and secretly, sometimes even openly, longed for a day when she might be discovered, featured in a television sitcom. Then she would move to Los Angeles, where he wouldn't have to go out to see her in strange, poorly written plays in strange little theaters with signs on the lobby walls that shocked him and too many young people trying desperately to look unique, memorable. If she were famous, he could sit in the comfort of his own apartment, at his favorite end of the sofa, on a regular schedule, say Tuesdays at 8:00 p.m. Howard's daughter was fond of telling her father to "get serious." He thought that was funny, but it got on his nerves, too. "Get serious" from a woman pushing thirty who lived in an endless parade of frivolous fantasy worlds. Even her real job was a fantasy. She did copyediting at an advertising agency, finding mistakes in ridiculous claims about unnecessary products. Not the big mistakes of advertising the stuff in the first place. She crossed the "t's" and dotted the "i's" on nonsense and lies. And she tells him to "get serious?"

Howard loved his daughter but he grew restless whenever

he had to spend more than a few minutes with her. The surprise product of a marriage that looked for a decade as if it would be a childless one, Stephanie had challenged Howard's love of routine. She was inherently chaotic, far more so than her mother, resisting all attempts at standardization. No matter what the books said, this baby decided to go to sleep some days at seven o'clock, others at eleven. Some days she took naps, other days she barely slept. She had favorite toys, abandoned them, returned to them, abandoned them again. One day it was her blanket she demanded, another her Piglet doll, another her stuffed bunny. The only routine she kept as an adult, at least as far as Howard could tell, one that both pleased and annoyed him, was checking up on her father. She'd insisted on giving him her old answering machine, when she went to Voice Mail, so he wouldn't miss any calls from her. (She knew he'd never spring for the modest cost of Voice Mail. "What do I need that for?" he'd say. "I never get any calls except from you.") She called three times a week. Often to tell him of some audition, some part she narrowly missed getting, some film that was shooting locally and needed extras, and did he want to come along? (No, he did not.) She was fond, too, of telling him he ought to get a computer: something to keep his mind active. Howard had resisted. "My mind's active enough," he would say.

"So what are you thinking about these days?" she'd counter.

"Just never you mind," was his stock reply.

To which hers was "Sorry, it doesn't work that way. You're my dad. I'm going to mind."

"You've got it backwards," Howard would grumble. "I'm the parent. You're the child. Stop trying to reverse roles on me."

No, he was doing fine, thank you very much, considering. Considering he'd been a widower now for six years,

considering he'd never really lived alone till then (having gone
directly to married life from army life, and before that, life as
the youngest in a large family. Considering that of his eight
older siblings, only one was still alive and she was in a nursing
home in Kansas City somewhere, smiling pleasantly at everyone, recognizing no one.

He had checked his watch — five minutes till curtain time —
and started to jog. The pain hit him just after the midpoint of
the bridge. "What's the meaning of this?" Howard asked his
heart, when it asserted itself into his awareness by knocking
on his rib cage with a sharp, sudden ache. It didn't stay sharp,
and it didn't travel down his arm, so Howard dared to hope
that his life was not yet over. He stood still for a few moments
till it subsided, then resumed his journey, but at a much slower
pace. Gingerly, he completed the bridge crossing. Cautiously,
he computed the distance yet to go and judged it against the
shortness of breath he still felt. Carefully, he stepped the last
two blocks to the theater. Gratefully, he noted that Portland
audiences were late and the show hadn't begun yet. He sank
into a seat and rested.

"Look, Bessie," he thought to his heart, which was still causing him a vague twinge now and then. "I know I haven't been
the best overall body a heart could have, but for Godsakes
don't leave me now. I gave up smoking eleven years ago already.
What more do you want?" Why Bessie? He didn't know. It just
seemed like the name to call her.

Maybe that was what got it started. Asking an open ended
question like that. Speaking to an internal organ by name. He
should have known better.

The show was not really a show. It was a whole collection
of little shows. All of them supposed to be about Spring, but
instead they were about everything else under the sun. The

one Howard's daughter was in, she played a tourist who interrupts a guy who's about to commit suicide by jumping from a scenic vista. She drives him nuts talking about her hangnail problem and he runs away from the edge. So she saves his life. Silly play. And nine more just as silly. But she told him not to leave after her play was over because it was rude. Can you beat that? He's the father. She's the daughter. And she's lecturing him on what is and isn't rude. Now that's rude.

The phone was ringing when he got into the house, which surprised him, because he had the answering machine set to pick up at two rings. He ignored it for ten, then gave in and picked it up.

"Howard, this is your Heart calling. Remember me?"

"My what?"

"Your Heart, Howard. What did you think I said?"

"Why do you sound like my mother?"

"Who else should I sound like? Think about that, Howard. Howard!"

"What? Who is this?"

"I told you. I'm your Heart."

"Yeah, yeah, okay." Some kind of pitch, Howard thought. Some kind of request to donate. They get more devious every day. "What do you want?"

"I want you to take better care of me. You scared me going over that bridge too fast today. I'm not used to your running, and that's because you sit around too much. And the fat, Howard. The bacon. Haven't you ever heard about cholesterol?"

"Of course I've heard about cholesterol. Who hasn't?"

"And what's yours?"

"How should I know?"

"My point exactly. You've never even gotten it tested."

"Who is this?" Howard was getting a little pissed.

"Stress is very bad for me, you know. And I get stressed when I get yelled at. Look," the voice said, "Just think about it. You need me. So all I'm asking is that you take care of me a little better, that's all. Is that too much to ask? Pick up the phone, call the doctor, get me checked out. Believe me, you'll thank me."

While Howard was trying to frame a response, the phone went dead. "Wait!" he said, but he was talking to a dial tone.

He dialed Stephanie. It wasn't entirely like her, but who else would pull a prank like that? He barely knew anyone else. Since Louisa had died, he stopped going to church (it was always something he did for her) and drifted away from getting together with their mutual friends (more and more of whom were surviving widows who made him feel too closely watched). There was no answer at Stephanie's. He called every ten minutes until it was time to go to bed, which he always did promptly after Jay Leno's monologue.

Howard didn't sleep well that night, but nonetheless awoke at the usual 5:45 a.m. In the kitchen, he replaced yesterday's coffee filter with a new one, and while the coffee brewed, he got the paper from the hallway and the sweetened, condensed milk from the refrigerator, which was his routine. Also routine was the fact that he got impatient with the dripping and poured his first cup before all the water had gone through the grounds. This always caused a slight spill of coffee onto the hot plate element of the coffee maker and the counter next to it, which Howard always noted, but only vaguely, vaguely making a mental note to wipe it up later, which he routinely forgot to do. The fact that Howard was a man of routine did not mean he was a man of fastidious housekeeping.

Howard was about to enjoy his morning coffee and

headlines when the phone rang. "Six o'clock?" Howard said it aloud because there was no one to hear him talking to himself. And had there been someone to hear it, he wouldn't have been talking to himself anyway. Living alone was like that. He put his coffee cup back on the table so he could give his full attention to the phone. He watched it ring. After two rings, the answering machine picked up, like it was supposed to. He heard his outgoing message, which was nothing if not succinct. "Leave a message," it said.

"Howard, this is Frank, your stomach calling. How about something in me before you send that slop my way? The acid is killing me."

By the time he got to the phone, the caller had hung up.

He called Stephanie, waking her up. She couldn't make sense out of what he was asking. "Forget it," he said. He hit *69 on his phone. Was told his call could not be completed as dialed. The next day he stopped at a phone store, bought and installed caller I.D.

So that's how it started. The caller I. D. turned out to be useless, even after he set it to accept only those calls that came from unblocked numbers. It always showed his own number as the origin of the call. If he let it ring, he heard a voice on the answering machine, and when he answered the phone, it spoke directly to him. It was never the same voice. If his heart had sounded like his mother, he had to figure the stomach was his maternal grandfather's voice. His paternal grandfather's voice was the gall bladder, his father's voice the lungs, and his sister who had been dead for thirty seven years was the liver. They each claimed a name, so in addition to Bessie and Frank, Howard got messages from Rudy, Chet, and Lucinda. None of them were actual family names. These body parts were just imitating his closest relatives. This struck Howard as a little on the tasteless side, but when he complained to them about it, they either ignored him or claimed not to know what he was taking about. Well, at least none of them had the temerity to sound like Louisa. As a rule, they tended, all of them, to be one-dimensional and humorless.

He considered throwing the answering machine away, but he knew Stephanie would worry about him. She worried about him anyway, and told him so with increasing frequency. "I'm worried about you, Dad. You never get out of the house, you never read anything, you never talk about anything like you're interested in it." She bought him a VCR and a gift certificate for the video store that was just a block from the house. He resisted, so she started bringing him videos to watch. Inspirational videos, starring senior citizens who go on kicky, quirky trips like whale watching and wilderness hiking and camping in cow fields and riding lawn mowers for hundreds of miles. Howard would forget to watch them until they were due back.

"I'm worried about you, Dad. You need to develop some kind of new interest. Why don't you take a computer class at the senior center?"

Between his internal organs and his daughter, Howard never heard the end of all the things that were wrong with him and his attitude. He began to pray, in an offhand not really believing in it sort of way, that his daughter would move somewhere far away. And he began to fear the day the voices would leave him. He preferred the company of his spleen, his pancreas, his appendix even to that of his daughter. But he was especially getting to be — fond isn't exactly the right word, but perhaps used to — Bessie. His heart. Sometimes, Howard would sit very still and listen for her beat. Sometimes, he wouldn't hear it or feel it and then he would panic and think perhaps he was a ghost, already dead. The panic would cause his pulse to quicken, and then he'd know he was still alive. Because his heart knew how to pound.

In the morning, he'd always greet Bessie. He knew she was the key to it all.

By the time Howard greeted his heart on this particular morning, he'd been hearing from various body parts for several months. Each had a complaint and none was shy about sharing. "You think I like breathing moldy air? Ever think about cleaning your kitchen?" "They don't call it rot gut for nothing, ya' know." "You trying to choke me or what?" "You want to know why I'm unmitigated, try looking in the mirror sometime."

So Howard was glad he was sitting down when he heard Stephanie's voice on the answering machine saying she called to tell him she might be moving. She had just gotten the lead in a very funny, very well written play that would be opening next month at Theater Space Ink and rumor had it an agent friend of one of the theater's big supporters would be up to see it. She had a good feeling about the whole thing, Stephanie said. An instinct that told her it was time to make the move to L.A. His daughter's message made him feel a little dizzy. He didn't want a goddam fall, a goddam broken hip leaving him accusatory messages. "You should have known better. You should have sat down. Now you've fallen and broken me. Is that what you want? To break me? After all the years I've worked for you?" No, a damn broken hip haunting his message machine would be too much. Enough was enough, with his heart, his liver, his prostate (named Dick, for Chrissake) and his lungs all nagging him. No need to add hipbones. The message went on. "I've bought a new laptop so I can travel light in case I get a touring gig. I think you should take my desktop and the computer hutch.

It'll give you something to do. I'll be over right after five to deliver it."

Bessie had a field day as they lugged it all up to Howard's apartment. She didn't even wait to leave a message on the answering machine. "You can't do this to me. You just can't. I'm not used to all this up the stairs down the stairs lift the desk put the desk down downstairs again lift the chair, up down up down. Don't take me for granted Howard. I'm better than that. Oh boy am I glad Louisa didn't live to see this. It would have killed her."

"Leave Louisa out of this," Howard growled.

"What?" Stephanie asked.

"Nothing," Howard hastened to reply.

That night, he noticed the blinking light signaling a message. It was Bessie again, telling him to check how fast she was ticking. He took his pulse. One hundred eighteen. Even though he'd been sitting quite still for an hour or more. One hundred eighteen.

Jesus. That's fast.

The phone rang.

"That does it," Bessie told him when he'd barely lifted the receiver to say hello. "You're going to the doctor first thing in the morning."

"But 118 isn't..." Howard began to protest, but Bessie would hear none of it.

"No ifs, ands, or buts about it," she interrupted.

"That's Dad's line," Howard protested, but his heart, having had its say, was silent. "Look, who is this?" It was time to get to the bottom of this extended and not very amusing practical joke. "Who are you? I demand to know!" All he could hear was the quietly labored sound of breathing. "Sonofabitch, stop stalking me!" Howard roared his frustration and slammed the phone down. A timid knock at the door. He startled, stared. The knock again. He put the chain on, opened the door just enough to peek out. It was Mrs. Crandall, from across the hall. "Are you all right, Howard? I was just coming back from my after dinner walk and thought I heard yelling in here, and I thought, why Howard lives alone. I hope no one has broken in to his apartment. Are you all right?"

"I'm fine, Mrs. Crandall. Thanks for looking in on me."

She looked expectant, as if there were more to the transaction than this. "Good night," Howard smiled and shut the door on the outrageously robust neighbor, fifteen years his senior.

The phone rang again. He refused to answer it. He heard the message nonetheless: "You know, Mrs. Crandall really knows how to take care of herself. You should take a page from her book." Howard hit the delete button and stomped into the kitchen.

He sat at his table and made a list of possibilities. At the head of one column he put his answering machine's initials. At the head of another he put his initials. Then he tried to remember the symbolic logic he'd learned forty-seven years before in his first year of college. IF -> THEN, he wrote above the headings. Under AM he wrote IF AM -> FIX AM. Under HB he wrote IF HB -> FIX HB. Back in column one he listed givens: AM is a machine. AM isn't alive. AM takes messages. Only alive (people) can leave messages. .: messages AM delivers are left by live people .: AM is not live. Then he drew a big X through the whole mess because he realized he was mixing metaphorical apples and oranges. Fruit salad, he muttered aloud to no one in particular. He began again, this time in the HB column. IF hear voices AND voices are not real THEN am crazy.

He didn't like the way it looked, so he tore the whole chart into shreds. I am NOT crazy, he affirmed to his reflection as he brushed his teeth that night. And as he lay in bed, waiting for sleep, he repeated to himself "I am not crazy, I am not crazy." He slept fitfully, dreaming of shadows and pursuits. When he woke up to urinate at 2 a.m. and again at 4 a.m. he reminded himself "I am not crazy." The next morning, when his Isles of Langerhans called, Howard threw in the towel. "I'm crazy," he announced to the picture of Louisa over the roll top desk. "I'm crazy as a loon." The Isles were still playing on the answering machine. They were singing some little ditty, sounding like the Chipmonks. "I'm crazy," Howard said again, only addressing the remark this time to the Isles.

"You're not crazy," they chittered back at him. "You just need a check up. Go see why we aren't functioning so well."

"We? We? Who do you mean we?"

That was the cue for the Isles to break into song:

> *We are the Isles of Langerhans*
> *We make you insulin*
> *If we get all exhausted*
> *Diabetes will kick in.*

"Ach!" Howard growled at the tiny singing things. "My blood sugar is fine."

"Is not," they chittered.

"Is too," he countered.

"Is not," they insisted.

"Is too!" he couldn't believe he was bickering with his Isles of Langerhans, but there you have it. He was. And they were getting on his last nerve. Which was probably about to declare itself and take his stomach's side in the question of whether he drank too much coffee.

"How do you know? How do you know?"

"I just do."

"Prove it. Prove it."

That's how it came to pass that Howard, to shut them up, turned to "Physicians" in his phone book and found a general practitioner who would accept new patients. An appointment was set with Dr. Patterson for the following Tuesday morning, 10:00 a.m. His answering machine was ecstatic. All his parts talked at once, gibble gabbling about how happy they were he was finally doing this. He put a sofa cushion over the answering machine so he could hear himself think, because adjusting the volume didn't seem to have any effect on these Weisenheimers.

"Is this the first time you've seen Doctor Patterson?" Howard noddded. "You'll need to fill out the medical history and emergency contact information, then bring it back to me. Do you have any other insurance? I'll need a copy of your card."

Howard looked in dismay at the pages of checklists. "This is a lot to fill out. I'm just here for a quick check up," he protested.

"It's just routine, take your time. Let me know if you need help."

What does she think, I'm too senile to fill out a few forms? Howard retreated to the furthest corner of the waiting room and began filling in the blanks. The checklist was a cinch. He knew the heart disease was on his mother's side and the cancer was on his father's. He didn't smoke. Anymore. And rarely drank. He was acing this. Then the questions started in with how well does he sleep? Does he have night sweats? Does he frequently get up during the night to urinate? Does he have disturbing dreams? Howard stared at the questions. When the perky little nurse checked back in with him to see if he was finished, he was still staring.

"Everything all right?"

"What? Oh, yes. I didn't get this quite finished."

"That's all right. The nurse practitioner can go over it with you."

"The good news," said Doctor Patterson, as he pried Howard's mouth open the better to peer at his throat, "is you stopped smoking long enough ago that it has a beneficial effect on your life expectancy."

"Tell that to Bessie," Howard gargled around the tongue depressor.

"Is that your wife?"

Howard flushed. "My wife's dead."

"Oh," the good doctor said, with trained compassion in his voice. "Is Bessie a special friend then?"

"You could say that." Howard knew his tone was rude, but he didn't care. He wanted to put a stop to this line of inquiry immediately.

He left after promising to call the office in a week for the results of his lab tests. The doctor had offered to call him, but Howard said he'd prefer to call in. How will I know, he was thinking, that a message on that machine is legit? It could be some practical joke my spleen decides to play on me.

That night, Howard watched the disk defragmenter. Stephanie's old computer came with her advice that he should defrag it before using it. She'd showed him how, and that's where matters had sat since the day they'd moved it in and set it up. There was a button you could click on to see the legend. Sure, thought Howard, why not?

The legend was color coded. Each color meant something. Belongs at the beginning of a drive. Belongs in the middle of a drive. Belongs at the end of the drive. Optimized. Free space. Data that will not be moved. Bad area of disk. Data currently

being read. Data currently being written. The boxes flashed
by, each representing one disk cluster. Howard noticed great
expanses of free space. White, interrupted by short strings of
things that belonged somewhere else. Is this somehow a metaphor for him? he wondered. Then suddenly gone, in a flash
of greens and the total screen was white for a moment. Is
this like my life passing in front of me, Howard thought, and
now its gone and I'm a blank slate again? A *tabula rasa?* Now
where did that idea come from? A philosophy class, 55 years
before when Howard attended his first and only year of college. Why was he suddenly remembering bits of phrases from
that class? *Tabula rasa.* Short nasty, brutish and mean. The
sun will rise tomorrow. Probably. And still he was only 31%
defragmented. Still very fragmented. Fragmented. Still. Very.
Not much optimized data in this old boy. The rhythm of the
defrag tool chugging away sounded like drums in the park, if
he blurred the sound a bit. A 4/4 rhythm, but with syncopa-
tion. Thoughts tried to enter his brain but he recognized them
as irritations and rejected them. Perry Como. Althea Gibson.
Babe Didrickson Zaharis. Free Willy. Remedial reading. 33%
complete, 33, the year that Christ died.

   And suddenly the drive contents changed. Restarted. Reading drive information, the computer told him. The screen
blanked out and the process began again at the beginning, a
little faster this time. Howard blurred his eyes and the pale
blue blocs were suddenly thrown into the third dimension.
Deep, behind the darker blues. Like those hidden picture
things.

   It's like a music box, Howard thought. The patterns of
blocks produce sound syncopations and regular beats, like one
of the little metal player piano type things that makes a music
box work. It was soothing; it made Howard drowsy.

"Dad, pick up the phone. Dad! Come on, answer the phone. It's me, Stephanie."

Howard forced his eyes to open and sat up from the slump he'd slept in by the computer. His back was killing him, and there was a crick in his neck. The answering machine was speaking to him in what sounded suspiciously like Stephanie's voice, but this was her opening week so she was in rehearsals till late every night and wouldn't be calling so early in the morning. He figured it was another body part. Maybe the muscles were going to start in on him, chew him out for sleeping at the computer like that instead of going to bed.

"I know you're there."

He stumbled across the room and eased himself down onto the sofa before resting his tired head against the telephone receiver. "Which part is it?" he asked.

"How did you know?"

"Know what?"

"That I'm calling you about a part?"

"I didn't." It was Stephanie. "I thought you were someone else."

"Who?"

"Nobody."

"Who? Who did you think I was, Dad?"

"Nobody."

"You have a lady friend you haven't told me about?"

"Stephanie, stop it. Why did you call?"

"I have a part for you."

"What?"

"A part. In a play. We need you to take over a part. It's not big, but it's very important. There's just one line. Mostly you sit in a big chair and hide behind a newspaper."

"Stephanie, what are you talking about?"

"The play I'm in, Dad. We open tonight, and the guy who was doing the part crapped out on us."

"Get serious, Stephanie."

"I'm totally serious, Dad. Listen, it's really important to me to have our opening night go well. There's an agent—Anita Bankhaven—she's coming to see the show and if she likes what she sees she might sign me on."

"Sign you on what?"

"Take me on as a client. Represent me. Get me auditions."

"I don't see what this has to do with me."

"There's this part, I told you. We need someone to fill in. You'd be perfect. Dad, I told everyone you'd do it. The stage manager ran a script for you. He's at work all day, but he'll meet you at 6:30 tonight to show you your stage directions and line. We won't have time for a run-through, but it's really totally simple."

"Have you lost your mind?"

"Dad, it'll be great for you. You sit around in that musty apartment all day, you never get out and when you do, you never get more than four blocks from home. This will be fun. It'll be a kick. The part is an old guy who sits around all day behind his newspaper and the whole play goes on all around him until at the very end he lowers his paper and says, 'I'm not dead yet.' It's hilarious. Trust me."

"And there's nobody in the entire city who can do this part? I find it hard to believe."

"We called everyone we could think of and no one's available. But I swear none of them would understand the character the way you will. Dad, this is important. If Anita Bankhaven likes my work it could lead to something really big."

"Your work will be fine no matter who you get to do the sit

in the chair and say a one line thing. Call Seattle. Don't they have actors up there? It's only a three hour drive."

"Dad, please. I want you to do this for me. Please. It's not like I've ever asked for much."

"You asked for a private room when you went to OSU."

"Yeah, but I didn't get it. I had three roommates all through college, remember?"

"You asked for a new car for your graduation present."

"And you got me a '74 from the police auction."

"It ran well, didn't it?"

"Get serious."

"You asked—" Howard hesitated. What had she ever asked for? It was true. Not much. She'd always been the kind of child who made you guess what she wanted because she'd never say it. She'd never explicitly invited him to see her perform even. She just called and said "I've got a comp ticket for you if you want it." And he'd go. There was a bus that stopped in front of his building and if he left in time, he could transfer to the bus that crossed the bridge. These days, since that first jolt from Bessie, he preferred not to walk it.

"Dad, look, you were going to come to opening night anyway, right? So the only thing that's different is you'll be on the stage instead of in the audience. Promise me you'll be at the theater by 6:30. Barry will go over the script with you and the director will talk you through it and give you a couple of notes and you'll do fine." Howard heard a hint of Louisa's voice in Stephanie's pleading tone, and gave in.

"I'll do it tonight. Tomorrow you find someone to take over."

"Thank you, Dad. Dad?"

"What?"

"I love you."

It wasn't something Howard and Stephanie generally said

to one another. It made him flush and grow clumsy and gruff. "Yeah. What am I supposed to wear?"

The director was a young woman of appalling energy named Mariah. She told Howard it was *fabulous* that he was willing to take on the part, that she thanked him *so* much, and knew he would be *terrific*. They had ten minutes to talk over the play and Howard's role in it. I know you just sit there, Maria said, but it's important to know *why* you just sit there, you know what I mean? Because even in a small role, it's important to be *present* in the character. She said the world "present" as if it were the name of God. "So there you sit through two full acts behind the newspaper. What are you *doing* back there?"

"Well, the script says I'm reading the newspaper."

"But why? Are you a news hound? Are you avoiding doing the dishes? Are you reading the obituaries, looking for the name of a friend?"

"Well, I imagine I'd have to be doing a few different things if I'm sitting there for two hours. Unless it's the NY Times Sunday edition."

"That's *great*! That's *fabulous*. So tonight when you're onstage figure out and pay attention to all the different kinds of things you can be doing while it looks to the audience like you're just sitting there. I don't know if Stephanie told you or not, but Anita Bankhaven is going to be in the audience tonight. Plus the critics, of course. But don't let that make you nervous. All you need to do is come out in the blackout, take your seat and stay there until the end of Act I. Same in Act II, till your line. Cue for the line is Serena—that's Stephanie's character—asking 'Do you want some ice cream?' and you say…" she leaned over, expectant, inviting.

She sat in a distinctly masculine posture that made her

feminity the more vivid. Howard, distracted by the pose, delivered his line directly to her crotch. "I'm not dead yet."

"*Fabulous!*" she enthused. "You'll be *fabulous*. And then… you put the paper up again, the lights go down, you stand and join the others for a curtain call. Go right downstage left, straight down from your chair. Grab Stephanie's hand—she's going to be looking out for you—and just follow her lead. When she bows, you bow. And then follow her offstage, stage right."

In place in the dark on the stage, Howard was gripped with acute anxiety. What if his Body Parts—he'd begun to think of them that way, as a sort of named organization, perhaps even incorporated—started nagging him? His hands shook. As the lights came up, he tried desperately to still them. The paper rustled, the audience laughed. Stephanie, standing at the kitchen sink with her back to Howard, delivered her first line. "Do you want some coffee?" The audience howled. Howard got a grip on himself and quieted his hands. They howled again. And the play hadn't even really started yet.

"I'll have some," said the actor playing Howard's son, and the play was off and running with a kind of supercharged energy.

By the end of the first act, Howard had evoked laughter and applause by turning the pages three times, crossing his legs once, and uncrossing them once.

Backstage, the director was rhapsodic. "You are *fabulous*! Absolutely *fabulous*! What an *instinct*! Just keep it up!"

Howard was in a big of a daze. He wasn't sure what to keep up, other than the newspaper. He allowed himself to be gently pushed into his place for Act II by Barry, the young stage manager who'd showed him the script, explained where he needed to stand offstage and sit onstage, and who called him "Sir."

As Act II began, just the sight of him sitting in the chair again, in the same position, brought the house down. Ten minutes into the act, his arms beginning to tire from holding the newspaper up, he cautiously rested just his elbows on the arms of the chair. The audience chuckled. A little later, in the middle of a monologue by the actor playing his son — he still didn't know his real name, but in the play he was Roger — addressed to him, he came close to falling asleep. When he sagged a bit and then jerked himself back to attention, the audience clapped and guffawed. Then Stephanie entered with a can of mosquito repellant just as he gave in to an itch and scratched his left ankle with his right heel. The audience roared. He finally settled into a frozen pose, in almost a trance-like state, to await his cue. Immobile how, his very rigidity seemed to cause fits of giggles to erupt in the audience every now and again.

In his effort to stay awake and still, he focused on his daughter and gradually got used to hearing her addressed as Serena. The play revolved around Serena and Roger's relationship. Howard was surprised to hear how well she delivered her lines. He'd sat through quite a few plays she'd been in, but never had she gotten laughs like she was getting tonight. It was tempting to peek sometimes, too, when he heard laughter in the audience but neither she nor Roger nor any of the other three secondary characters were speaking. What was she doing?

At the opening night party, Stephanie hooked her arm through Howard's and pulled him across the room to meet Anita Bankhaven. Anita was, Howard noted in surprise, somewhere around his own age. She was with a friend, introduced as Peggy Entermann, a benefactor of Theater Space Ink. Anita raised her plastic glass of red wine in a toast. "Here's to genetics," she said. "It's very easy to see where Stephanie gets her sense of comic timing. And she tells me this is your first role? I can scarcely believe it."

Peggy agreed. "And here's to Dads," she added. "I think it's wonderful you were willing to step in and help out on such short notice. I understand the actor who was originally cast wasn't able to do it."

"Yes, well…" Howard wasn't used to so much attention from real people. He covered the awkward moment by lifting his beer bottle. "Here's to Theatre Space Ink."

"Here's to Theatre Space Ink," they all chorused.

They drank, and in that small silent space Stephanie was called to by someone on the other side of the room. Anita was accosted by an actor who had crashed the party in hopes of hand-delivering his resume to her. Howard and Peggy were left alone in the crowd.

"You must be very proud of your daughter," Peggy said.

Howard didn't know quite how to answer that, so he just stood there thinking. Was he proud of her? What did that mean, to be proud of one's child? What qualities would be grounds for pride? Had he ever thought about that? Peggy's words interrupted his impromptu reverie. "Aren't you?"

Howard saw the look on her face and found himself answering, to his astonishment, honestly. "I never much thought about it until just now. I think I am, yes. I think I'm proud of her that she kept at this in spite of me. I don't think I encouraged her very much. She was good tonight, wasn't she?"

"She was wonderful," Peggy agreed. She cocked her head a tiny bit and looked at him almost as if he were a museum exhibit. "You were, too."

Howard started to say "All I did was follow my orders," but

Bessie wouldn't let him. 'Just say thank you, Howard,' she hissed in his ear. "Thank you," he said.

Peggy smiled.

When Howard got home that night, he expected a raft of calls. Maybe one from his bladder griping about the beer (he'd indulged in four bottles). Maybe his lungs objecting to the smoke-filled atmosphere of the party. (You'd think people who made a living with their voices and bodies would take better care of them, Howard thought.) Maybe the Isles of Langerhans, bitching about the number of times he'd reached for the chocolate covered cherries on the treats table. But the phone was silent, and there were no messages.

He found his favorite spot on the sofa and settled in to watch Jay Leno's monologue. Tomorrow, he'd be back on stage. Mariah wouldn't hear of anyone else doing the part, he'd been so *fabulous*. Whaddya think of that, Bessie?" Howard asked, but Bessie wasn't talking, hadn't said a word all day save for the order to say "thank you."

He woke up during Conan, disturbed by sounds in the hallway. Hurried, urgent, rustling sounds. When he peeked through his peephole, he saw white-coated medical personnel. His first, irrational, dream state thought was that they were coming for him. Then one of them said "You hang on, Mrs. Crandall. Hang on." And off they went, rolling her down the hallway toward the elevator as fast as they could.

Howard made a quick stop in his bathroom, then proceeded to his bedroom. He caught his dead wife watching him from the framed photo on the bedstand. "What?" he asked the image. He could have sworn she smiled a little smile. A sort of Harrison Ford grimace. "What?" he asked again, but she wouldn't say.

He gave in, went to sleep. He was so tired he slept right through till 6:00.

In the morning, he put the coffee on and waited for the phone to ring. While the coffee brewed, he poured himself a bowl of cereal and made a mental note to buy some bananas. Someone at the party last night had said they were a good source of potassium.

When he opened his door to get the paper, he saw Mrs. Crandall's copy and remembered that she'd been taken away in the middle of the night. He brought hers in too. No sense leaving it there for someone to steal. He wondered where she was. Maybe after he read the paper he'd call a couple of hospitals. See if she was all right. Nah. He'd do it now, so he wouldn't have to wonder. What was her first name? Elisabeth.

The University Hospital was nearest and that's where she was. The receptionist connected him to ICU where the nurse wanted to know his relationship to the patient. "Are you a relative?"

"No, just her neighbor across the hall."

"She's resting comfortably."

"Is she going to be all right?"

"She should be able to come home in a week or so. Do you know if she has any family in the area?"

Howard was chagrined to realize he'd lived over half a decade on the same floor as Elisabeth Crandall, seen her several times a week, and had not a clue. "I really don't know," he said. "Are there visiting hours?" You couldn't leave a person in the hospital for a whole week without visiting.

He hadn't been inside that place for six years. Not since he'd sat by Louisa's bedside and watched her give up, bit by bit. It hadn't been a kind death, nor an expected one. Out on a walk one day, part of her health maintenance routine, Louisa stepped off a curb, stumbled, and fell. At first it seemed like a sprained ankle and a cut on the palm of her hand were the only consequences. A quick trip to the emergency room to tape her ankle and clean the cut should have been the end of it. But six weeks later she started to feel unwell. Vague, flu-like symptoms plagued her. She lost her appetite. She couldn't seem to get enough sleep. Her chest felt tight. By the time she allowed as how she probably should get in to see what was going on, it was too late. An antibiotic resistant bug had taken over her body. They put her on i.v. vancomycin, the last ditch drug, but the stress on her liver and kidneys just added to the insult. One night, while Howard kept vigil in the chair next to her bed, Louisa let go.

Howard remembered how the nurses had suggested keeping cut flowers out of her room. The water was a breeding ground for who knows what. He'd found a large card for her with a bouquet of paper flowers that popped out when you opened it, but never signed it, never delivered it, because the call saying she was fading fast had distracted him from anything other than just getting over there to the hospital.

The card was still in the store bag, in a box in the bedroom closet, where he always put anything he didn't know quite what else to do with. He hesitated for a second or two. It was, in some way, Louisa's — even if he'd never given it to her. But Bessie suggested Louisa wouldn't mind, and Howard agreed. He wasn't sure how to sign it. "Your neighbor" seemed stiff, yet obvious. "Regards" he rejected on the grounds that it sounded like a business memo. "Sincerely" struck him as too generic. "Yours" would be a lie. He wasn't hers. He settled for simply signing "Howard" across the bottom. Card and Mrs. Crandall's morning paper in hand, Howard headed to the hospital.

He was relieved that she was asleep when he got there. It

allowed him to leave the items with the nurse and get out of there. The stress of being back where he last saw his wife alive had caused Bessie to be in a bit of a flurry. Howard wanted to get away from the hospital, so he didn't sit down at the bus shelter in front where he normally would have. He walked a block first, and found an upscale coffee house. The kind Stephanie would hang out in. "I'll tell you what," he thought to Bessie. "We'll take it slow. Sit here for a while, have a cuppa." He took silence for consent. Nevertheless, when he stepped up to the counter, something prompted him to order decaf. The coffee was not bad. In fact, it was a damn sight better than the stuff he was used to drinking. He decided to buy a pound and try it at home.

Back out on the street, Howard checked the bus schedule. He'd just missed one. Twenty minutes. He might as well walk. It was a beautiful summer day, perfect for a stroll. He ambled down the street, enjoying the aroma of freshly ground coffee that wafted up from the bag in his hand. At the corner, he was somewhat taken aback to see an enormous hole in the ground. The sign said it was the future home of Excelsior Apartments, a luxury retirement community. Try as he might, he couldn't remember what had been there before. He stood for several minutes watching the men down at the bottom of the hole working on laying drainage pipes. "It's something, innit?" Another man had stopped to watch and spoke to Howard.

Howard glanced at the man and smiled. "Yes, it surely is." The man shook his head and walked on down the street.

Howard watched for another minute or so, then walked on. The route home took him by the supermarket, so he stopped in to pick up the bananas. He considered waiting for a bus again, but he was already half way home. "I'll just take her easy," he thought to Bessie. "You let me know if it's too much and I'll hop on the bus."

The light on the answering machine was blinking. Howard took his time getting to it. First he went to the kitchen. He tossed the leftover coffee in the coffee pot, filled a filter with the new stuff, and poured the water. The counter was more than a little crusty, so while he waited for the new pot of Bird Friendly Swiss Water Process Rain Forest Fair Trade Decaf to brew, he wiped up the accumulated spills of…could he even remember how long ago he'd last wiped the counter down? He could not. Surely, he'd done it at least a few times over the past six years. Or maybe that was something Stephanie did when she stopped by.

The coffee was still dripping so he peeled and ate a banana. "See that, Frank? Ya' happy?" he said to his stomach. When the coffee was ready, Howard poured a cup and took it back to the living room. He tasted it. Yep, it really did taste better than the stuff he'd been buying on sale in three pound tins. He tossed a mental note in the direction of his nervous system. "No need to get jittery," he told it. "This is decaf."

Sitting in his usual spot, he was aware suddenly of how it sagged compared to the rest of the sofa. He scooted a little to his right, testing a different place in the cushions, where the foam was still firm, or at least not so compressed it was beginning to crumble.

There were two messages. The first from Stephanie, rushed and aglow with the previous night's triumphant opening. "Hi, Dad, I've got an audition for the new satellite radio thing? I say 'Get serious. Get Sirius.' Or something like that. I've never even heard of satellite radio before, have you? Did you read the review? 'A work of comic genius with a cast to match?' I still can't believe how well it all came together last night. You're a natural, Dad. You should go to the auditions for *I'm Not Rap-paport* at Center Stage. Seriously. I'll be down in L.A. by then, but if you get a part I'll definitely come back up for your open-ing night. Gotta get back to work now. See you tonight."

He fully expected the next message to be from Bessie. Or maybe Frank. Or the Isles. But it was a new voice — yet oddly familiar. "Hello, Howard, I hope I'm not calling too early." Obviously not a Body Part, Howard thought. A Body Part would never apologize for calling too early.

"I just wanted to tell you again how very much I enjoyed your performance last night."

"Who is this?" Howard asked out of habit, expecting inter-action.

"I'm having a little get together next Tuesday for a few friends of Theater Space Ink, and I do hope you'll join us."

"Who *is* this?" Howard asked again.

"You can let Barry know tonight. He's keeping track of the guest list for me."

"Who….Is…..This?" Howard demanded.

"I'm just about to go out to Cannon Beach until Monday, so I won't get to see you perform again tonight. But I know you'll be wonderful. I…" The message was cut short. Howard's answering machine was set for thirty seconds. An emphatic static-filled beep announced the end of the messages. There would not be a third. Whoever it was hadn't called back.

He hit the replay button and listened again. Of course. It was Peggy whatsername. He smiled, hit the replay button once more, and settled back to listen.

Independence Day

THEY TALK ABOUT her as if she's deaf. Especially her daughter-in-law Marilyn, on the phone as usual chatting with one friend or another: "She's doing as well as can be expected. No, it wasn't a surprise, but you know you're never really ready for something like that. Yes, he'd been sick for over a year. Well, the last three or four months were pretty rough. Fifty-one years they'd been married. They'd known each other since they were in high school, isn't that something? Yes, we thought it would be best for her to move in with us. Oh no, her memory's fine, thank God. It's just you know what they say about old people and isolation. They can get depressed and stop taking care of themselves. Now that she doesn't have Grandpa to keep her busy, we just don't want her at loose ends. This way the kids will get to know their grandmother better and they'll keep her entertained. Yes, there's that to be grateful for: they'd already downsized and gotten rid of a lot of their old stuff. It's a small house, not the one Petey and the rest grew up in so none of them have any real attachment to it. That's why we brought her here right away. We certainly didn't want to leave her all by herself, and there isn't really room for us to stay there with her. Besides, the kids are closer to day camp and all their friends in the neighborhood this way."

A few feet away, fully within earshot of Marilyn's well-intentioned prattle, Tilda snorts. Whether her children are attached to the house or not is irrelevant. She is herself quite attached to it. That is all that matters. And *of course* there isn't room. That is the whole point. For her and Jack to have had a little peace and quiet after raising five children (one of them married to the doting daughter-in-law who is presuming to rearrange her life for her at this very moment), eight grandchildren, and two great-grandchildren with a third on the way. Not that she sees much of the great-grandkids. That's Sadie's branch. The child who rebelled, the middle one who ran off before she graduated and came back just once, when her daughter Leesa was less than two. Then Leesa follows in her mother's footsteps and elopes with what's his name? Dan. They live with his parents. All six in a double-wide: can you imagine? The parents, Leesa and Dan, and the two little ones. Girls, named Paris and Tokyo for goodness sake. Who knows how soon they'll get knocked up and dragged down too? And now another one in the oven. Probably about to be named Cape Town or Kabul.

Jack Jr., the oldest, was always the most practical, sensible one. He waited till he finished his degree to leave home and get married. His wife Sharon is nice enough. His three, the second set of grandkids, all got scholarships. A good thing, too, since he and Sharon really couldn't afford the fancy private prep school they'd sent the kids to and had more than once hit Grandma Tilda up for sizable loans. Might as well call them gifts. They live halfway across the country so except for the day of the funeral, she hasn't seen them in three years.

Margie is the third child she doesn't see much of. Works in the middle of some forest out west. Lives in a little cabin all by herself. Says she likes her independence. Tilda can see that. Not the part about living out in the middle of all those trees and bugs, but being independent.

Tilda has never been independent. Went right from high school to marrying Jack. They hadn't spent a night away from one another since their wedding night except when she had the babies. Nowadays they bring the husbands right in and let them stay there in the hospital room. Not back then. And after Jack Jr., she had to admit she looked forward to a few days of bed rest and solitude each time another baby came along.

Especially the last two. A bonus crop as her husband had called them. Petey and Penny, twins born when she didn't even expect a single additional child. And now here's Penny married to Martin with Samantha, Hillary and the baby Jason; and Petey and Marilyn with little Jessica. It's a chore just to keep the names all straight. The twins live just a few blocks apart, too, as close as they ever were, so they get together quite a bit and the children...well, the noise they make could wake the dead.

Like this afternoon.

They'd had a 4th of July parade for her benefit, marching through the house banging pots and pans, blowing kazoos, and shouting HAPPY INDEPENDENCE DAY at the tops of their little lungs. Announcing hot dogs and potato salad in the yard.

She knew they meant well. Ah, but that was the trap, wasn't it? To go along with the plans of anyone who meant well, no matter what you really preferred to do? Jack meant well when he said no wife of his would ever have to work: that he liked her in the kitchen where she could have cookies and milk ready for the kids after school. The counselor who told her she had to change the lock on her own teenage daughter, show her a little "tough love," meant well. It didn't seem to trouble the counselor that Sadie, rather than seeing the light, rode off on the back of her boyfriend's Harley and had barely said two sentences to her mother since. Her daughter-in-law Marilyn, Petey's wife, meant well when she grabbed her by the elbow after the funeral service two weeks ago and steered her

into their SUV telling her that there was no way they'd let her
stay alone at her house at a time like this. Marilyn's friends
meant well with their incessant inquiries about her mental
health, and Marilyn meant well fielding them as if Tilda herself were incapable of speech. And yes, the children meant well
tromping through the house making that gawdawful racket
they called an Independence Day Parade and tugging at her
sleeves to take her out into the back yard. If everyone meant
so darned well, why did she feel so positively ill?

There, amid the generations and the neighbors, she'd
pushed bits of potato around on her plastic plate and pondered. How much would a cab cost to get her back home?
She wondered how the nasturtiums she'd planted in the
window boxes were doing, and whether the neighbor boy
Petey had hired to water them and cut the lawn was really
getting over often enough. She missed the bird feeder in the
back yard, where a pair of cardinals had courted earlier in the
year. They're probably mad at me for not putting any seed out
since mid-June, she thought.

The neighbors were relentlessly pleasant. "I bet you're
enjoying getting to see your grandkids every day." "I know
Marilyn and Pete are certainly happy to have you here. You
don't often see a daughter-in-law so fond of her mother-in-
law." "Jessica sure is proud to have her Grandma living with
her." "Penny says her kids are thrilled to have Grandma here
in West Falls so close by. She says it gives them more of an
excuse to visit their cousin Jessica. They just adore that little
girl." "Only six and smart as a whip, isn't she?" "She must take
after her grandmother."

Tilda stood with a noncommittal smile on her face enduring the neighbors' palaver while her mind wandered and
fretted. They've got it all planned out. The Little League games,

summer dance camp recitals, grandparent's day at school. Tilda thought lovingly of her tiny yard. Not big enough to entertain the extended family, let alone half the neighborhood.

How well is she doing? Marilyn's assurances to her vast network of friends notwithstanding, Tilda isn't sure.

By nine-thirty, plans are underway to load into the cars with lemonade for the kids, beer for the adults, and blankets and insect repellant for all, to head to the county park for the fireworks. It will reportedly be the most spectacular display ever.

Tilda insists she is tired. Her hip is bothering her. She will be just fine alone. They are to go on to the fireworks. ALL of them. She won't HEAR of anyone skipping it on her behalf. She is going to settle into the rocking chair and read *John Adams*. She's been meaning to for years—Petey told her she'd love it—and this is a perfect evening to begin. Really. They must all go. GO.

She stands at the window for a moment after they've pulled out of the driveway, awash in an odd thrill. This is it. The first time in five years she is actually alone. Jack, once he'd retired, had never left the house unless it was to go with her to do shopping, or twice a year attend church services, or drive over to visit the kids. Doting to a T. She had had to start locking the bathroom door just to get a few minutes of privacy. Then when he got sick, she couldn't leave him alone, even to shop. Marilyn insisted on dropping by with everything she needed. Except solitude. But now she is alone. Absolutely alone. She remembers a dream she used to have when she was ten or eleven that she could fly. That's how she feels at this moment: gliding on possibilities. Flying high. Unattached, untethered. Alone. Gloriously alone.

What can she do alone? She can sing! She belts out a few

bars of "Oh, What a Beautiful Morning." As she sings about everything going her way, she begins to wonder. What is that? What would be her way? Not her and Jack's way. Not Grandma Tilda's way. Just her way. "I gotta be me," she croons to the deliciously empty space around her.

The *John Adams* book sits fat, pompous and accusing on the end table. "Oh, shut up," she tells it. "I'll get back to you in good time if and when I feel like it."

What she really wants to do is paint. It comes up inchoate, clamoring, bedazzling and confusing her. Paint what? She doesn't know. She just wants to make her mark on something.

Jessica has an easel in her room, and a shelf full of art supplies: brushes, watercolors, a beginner's set of acrylics, and finger paints. Tilda knows, because she got them for her granddaughter last Christmas, and has noticed they've hardly been used. She takes the oversized pad of sturdy paper from the easel, most of its sheets still expanses of empty white, and carries it out to the kitchen table. But which paints to use? Let's start at the very beginning, she hums the tune as she retrieves the pots of finger paints, opens them all, and dips into a jar.

The first painting is blue. She splats her hands on the paper, and pulls them away to see the shapes she's made. The next painting is purple. Spirals of purple. Steadily, she paints her way through the pad of paper, testing color combinations and effects, humming and whistling a blurry medley of old Broadway show tunes. Tonight, tonight, dream the impossible dream, climb every mountain, bet your pretty neck I'm bustin' out all over coming up roses...

They find her there at eleven, staring at the table full of paintings, a cup of chamomile tea in hand. Petey, Marilyn, Penny, Martin, Samantha, Hillary, Jason, and Jessica tumble through the door, the baby asleep in his mother's arms, the rest still gibble-gabbling about the fireworks display. She raises her head from contemplating the riotous colors long enough to say hello to them all, and to tell them firmly, lovingly, that she'll be going home tomorrow, right after breakfast. "But Mom!" "Grandma!" "Mother!" "Tilda!" "Gammaw!"

Jason wakes up and begins to cry. Penny jostles the infant and pleads with her mother. "You really just got here! Two weeks isn't enough time to settle in. Give it time!" Martin coughs. Petey and Marilyn move in to stand on either side of her, as if she's about to make a dash for it right at this very moment.

Marilyn rubs her shoulders. "Mom, you're still grieving. You're upset. Think about it."

Samantha is stricken. "Grandma? Aren't you going to come to my soccer game tomorrow?" Hillary just toddles over to Tilda to grab her by the thigh and cling tight. Tilda strokes her head.

It is Jessica who understands. "Cool," she says, admiring one of the paintings: slashes of red and yellow that blend and swirl into outrageously orange whirlpools of color. She lifts the paper with infinite care and takes it to the refrigerator, affixing it to the surface with bright blue fridge magnets. "Gram, you can use my paints any time you want to visit."

Tilda smiles at her. "A little child," she says to the others, "shall lead them. Goodnight, dears." She begins to gather up the rest of the paintings, but is interrupted by Samantha.

"Can I have the blue one?"

"Of course," she tells her.

Hillary points to the purple swirly one. Tilda hands it to her.

"I'd like the yellow and green one too," Samantha says, "for next to Jason's crib."

"It's yours," she answers.

When the paintings have all been claimed and all have said their good nights, Tilda stands, shakes out her glitchy hip, surveys this loving, cozy home then, whistling a happy tune, makes her way to the guest room to pack her bag and be ready for the new day.

The Ache of It

MAXIE KEEPS TELLING everyone I'm cured. It's not exactly the truth. There's an ache in my side that just won't quit, and pardon my French, but I feel like shit. What's true is I didn't die yet.

Remember that old song? "All Or Nothin'?" That's Maxie. For her, I'm either dead or I'm fine. She "cain't be in between." This extends to everything she does and everything she thinks.

I try not to let it get to me. Even when she decided that our previously life-long friends Joe and Laura Porter are suddenly unfit to associate with. Me, I'm different. When Joe was indicted for insurance fraud—well, let's just say I understood how he could let things get out of hand like that. A fellow gets his back to the wall, wants to save face, next thing you know he can kiss his ass good-bye. Sure, I can understand that. If it weren't for Maxie, I'd still go golfing with Joe. If I could still swing a golf club. And I couldn't see where Laura had a damn thing to do with it. Yeah, she always had the little pharmacy out front, still has, but I don't think she ever knew the deals he was making in the back. Why should she know? And Joe never cheated his customers. It was the company he overbilled a little. Me, I make a distinction between trying to get a little something from the company you've been working your butt off for over forty years and taking from a customer needs it. Not Maxie. So if she didn't want to see them, well, I hadda respect she had her reasons. Like I said, all or nothin' with her. They're our best friends forty-some years, or they're nobody to us at all.

For her it's like it was *us* he defrauded. But this I will say for Joe Porter: in fifty-eight years he never once cheated me. Everything he ever sold me I paid a fair price for, even when we were kids. In fact some of his sales, I got great bargains. Like the autographed Jackie Robinson baseball card that I sold last year for a couple thousand bucks.

'Course I couldn't tell her about that. 'Cause then I woulda hadda tell her why I needed two thousand bucks in the first place. See, she never knew I had the collection to begin with. There are certain things I like to keep to myself, and my old baseball collection is one of them. The state of my bowels is another. I did not appreciate the way the nurses were always telling each other whether I'd taken a dump or not. But I'm getting off the subject here. The subject was Maxie.

So anyway, she spent all last month telling everyone I was dying. I guess I did give her a scare. But Maxie's what you might call super organized. She started making all the funeral arrangements. She cancelled my car insurance. She ordered my coffin. She practically wrote my obit for the Journal-Trib.

Then when she comes in three weeks ago Monday after the surgery they really didn't expect me to survive and there I am awake, you know what she says? "Oh my god you're alive. What am I gonna tell everyone?"

"That I'm alive," I suggest.

"I gotta cancel the service," she says.

"What service?" I say.

"Your Memorial," she says.

At first, I thought maybe it was the drugs. I thought I was just having some kind of very peculiar dream. They get you on some powerful drugs in those hospitals, can cause hallucinations, delusions, confusions, whatnot. But this is no dream. Turns out she's reserved the brand new community center for a memorial service. Put a notice in the neighborhood news-letter. And hadda put down a non-refundable deposit. Quite a sizeable one at that.

"You usually can't get a decent space on such short notice," she tells me. "We were very lucky."

"Well, excuse me for living," I say, "and screwing up your schedule."

She looks at me with a —how can I describe it?—a fond, calculating look that frankly worries me. I've seen this look before. It means she's hatching a plot. "It's all right," she says, "we'll have a celebration instead."

"Of what?"

"Of your recovery," she says. "What do you think?"

"Maxie," I say. I'm trying to be patient, but this is maybe the biggest test ever in a relationship that has tested me fifty-one years. "I'm not recovered. I'm just barely alive. I got tubes where I oughtta have tracts. I've got stitches and staples and I feel like shit. What in God's name is there to celebrate?" I mean, how am I supposed to tell her I'm only alive because I don't have the guts to die? That's not the sort of thing it's easy to tell a person, let alone that person is your wife of over half a century. Okay, I know, I know they got the tumor and they say they think they got it all and they say I'm too old for it to grow back fast anyway. I say what the hell do they know?

"Sal, Sal, Sal," she says. I'm always in trouble when she says my name three times like that. Not trouble like I did some-thing wrong, but trouble like she's going to do something for me and I'm going to wish she hadn't.

Like the time "Sal, Sal, Sal, you need a trim" which I didn't and told her as much but next thing you know she's got the scissors out causing a catastrophe to my remaining hair which takes three weeks plus the best cut Winston my barber can figure out to do which costs me plenty more believe me than the usual shave and a haircut two bits.

"Sal, Sal, Sal, you know you need to keep busy when you're retired, or you'll just waste away," so alluva sudden I'm getting a bowling ball for Christmas and I gotta spend money for the special shoes and the special this and the special that, and first night at the lanes I throw my back out so I still can't stand up straight without I get a stabbing pain.

You get the picture. She says my name like that, I'm in trouble.

So, "Sal, Sal, Sal," she's saying. "We gotta change your diet. And tomorrow you start walking, too, just a little at first, not too much. I bet you won't even get winded now you're gonna give up tobacco. We'll get you back into shape."

"What?" I can hear my voice. Listless. Maybe a little plaintive, even. Usually she would notice that and ask me what's wrong. But she doesn't want to know what's wrong this time, because what's wrong is what she's doing. For Maxie, ignorance is bliss. Or at least an excuse to keep going until somebody stops her.

"Sally, we're gonna make sure this is a Full Recovery we're celebrating. We're gonna get you on a Program." This is even worse, when she calls me Sally and starts talking like her nouns are capitalized.

So today is the Memorial Day Parade. I am being paraded. Maxie says, "Stop saying that. You make it sound like you're a Macy's hot air balloon or something." I say I feel like I am. Then she gets that "you have wounded me deeply and if I die tonight boy won't you be sorry unless you apologize to me right now I mean it" look. So I tell her I'm sorry. She gives me her "all right this time, but don't push your luck" look and runs off to tell the caterer it's time to bring the dessert, like they don't know this. Like it's not their job to know this.

Everyone is here. Except Joe and Laura. He's probably sitting on the couch watching Tiger Woods and she's I bet standing behind that counter, still counting out the tablets. She can't afford to retire now with all the legal bills coming in. Can you imagine? Seventy-four and still working every day? It's a damned shame, is what it is.

Anyway, Louis and Miriam are here. They're just back from visiting their new great-grandson in Tucson and he's spouting the poetry about it. "Childhood," he says, "is the kingdom where nobody dies." Louis used to teach women's poetry and literature, and he's got a quote for every occasion.

"Emily Dickinson?" Miriam's the only one really listens to him much. She shills for him.

"Edna St. Vincent Millay," he says.

"Oh," she says, and excuses herself to go to the whaddyacallit, the powder room.

Maxie's brother The Other Louie is here. I call him The Other Louie because my best friend in life Louis got there first with the Louie, even though he hasn't been Louie since high school. The Other Louie tells me I look fabulous. I tell him he needs to get his trifocals adjusted. My sister Mary is here. She really does look fabulous, but she's supposed to, right, because she's the youngest. The official word is Teresa has a little cold, nothing to worry about, but the nurses thought she'd be better off not going out until she's feeling well again. Actually, Maxie told Mary leave Teresa at the Home, because she wouldn't remember any of us anyway and Maxie thinks that would depress me. She doesn't know I know this. She thought I was dozing on the sofa the whole time she was setting this up with Mary. All these years, and she still doesn't know I'm usually not dozing when I'm dozing. I'm usually avoiding conversation.

My cousin Ruth is here. Boy, does she look terrible. Ralphie died what? Less than a year ago from the lung cancer, so what does she do as soon as he's buried? You guessed it. And hadn't had a cigarette since he was diagnosed, which was the same day coincidentally Joe was indicted. I remember because Maxie always talks about bad news comes in threes and the next night the police called to say they found Teresa walking around 2:00 a.m. in her nightgown and we hadda put her in the Home. What makes a smart woman like Ruth start smoking again when she's finally managed to stop? Now I'm stopped, I'll tell you, I plan to stay stopped. So can somebody please explain that to me why anyone would start up again knowing what we now know about this stuff? I'll never understand it, not if I live a hundred years.

Which is what Maxie proposes I do. Maxie's a little younger than I am, and she hates being alone. You could maybe go so far as to say she's terrified of it. She wants me to live to a hundred so she's guaranteed companionship. Didn't you ever hear of the merry widow? I ask her. She tells me that's not funny. She's written a song to the tune of "A Hundred Bottles of Beer on the Wall." "A hundred years to live, my Sal; a hundred years to live. If you don't stick around that long, you'll irritate your wife, ol' pal." Good god, Maxie, I tell her. That's eighteen more years. And I already feel like shit. You want me to go through eighteen more years of that?

"Your attitude stinks," she tells me.

Attitude, schmatitude, I say. A good attitude is highly overrated. I worked with a fellow back before the war had the best attitude of anyone I ever met. Dispatcher. The patience of Job, that guy had. Never a bad word for anyone, always cheerful, the kind of guy who'd loan you five and if you couldn't pay him back he'd just forget about it and loan you ten the next week so's you should have some left over this time. Got polio and died before he was thirty.

So anyway, except for Teresa, Joe, and Laura, they're all here, the family, the close friends, the neighbors, the not so close friends, the casual acquaintances. And the waiters, who I notice are all Jamaican, which I guess is because the caterer Maxie usually gets for a party was booked so they referred her to this new outfit, and I must say they did a pretty good job of it, are putting *tira misu* in front of us, filling our coffee cups, and handing us each a plastic glass of champagne, so any minute now people are going to toast me and roast me. Sal, they'll say, is a truly great guy. Then Harry will tell about the time they fooled me with the yellow foot joke. Which I gotta admit was a pretty good trick. I swear to God, made me think I had some jungle rot was gonna eat my feet off. This is the way he will exact revenge for the time he got his boots glued to the floor, which was priceless, I only wish we'da had video in those days. The Other Louie will claim I steered him away from buying Microsoft in 1984. He'll say I was unduly influenced by George Orwell, who, if you want to know the truth, I have not read to this day, besides which, Microsoft did not go public until 1986, but try telling that to The Other Louie. Melinda will tell everyone for the umpteenth hundredth time how I got her to the hospital when Barbara was born because Jack was ordered to report for his physical that same day, and then she'll cry and Jack will pat her arm. Mary will tell them I taught her how to read when the teacher couldn't. Louis will recite a poem. Miriam will ask if it's Emily Dickinson. He'll say it is. She'll be happy she guessed right. Ruth will just nod at everything everyone else says and she'll cry too, and Maxie

will get some Kleenex for her. The only thing is I won't get
a good cigar from Joe like I used to. It's a Joe-free party, and
supposed to be smoke-free, too, except Ruth steps into the
bathroom and you see the edge of the towel under the door I
swear to God just like we were back in junior high school and
you go in after her and the room stinks like smoke and that
stinky sweet air freshener.

Listen, I know how she feels. I mean, who am I kiddin'?
Truth is, it's only been since I went to the hospital I stopped
and I'm dying for a cigarette, a pipe, anything, but Maxie won't
let me.

How will she manage when I'm gone? Who will she
manage?

She must have invited everyone we ever met to this little
shindig. Must be over a hundred people here, not counting the
waiters. The close ones, friends and relations, she's got them all
at this front table. I hate to think what this must be costing us.

My god, we're old. We're old. Louis is 85 plus two at 80 plus
Helen who's at least 83 and four of us all born 1922 makes 652
and Maxie's 78 and...she's looking at me like I'm supposed to
do something. Did she just introduce me? They're all looking
at me. My dear friends. My dear old friends. I guess I'm supposed to talk now.

"My dear friends. I was just sitting here adding up our ages
and I lost count after six hundred fifty two. Not because I
have lost the ability to add, but because I was distracted by
your attention. You know, sometimes, no matter what we plan
to say, what we really say comes out entirely different, if you
know what I mean."

They all nod. Of course they know what I mean. They're
all like me, losing their memories, forgetting where they left
their keys, their glasses, their teeth. They've all got aches and

pains like me, the kind you get so used to if you wake up in
the morning without 'em you figure you musta died during
the night.

"But of course you can't know what I mean because I haven't
said it yet. And if it comes out different who would know
anyway, right?" Now they're starting to look worried. They
may be old, but they still know an old guy making no sense
when they see it. I figure I better keep talking.

"Louis, my oldest and I do mean oldest friend here. Remember when we used to go down to see the Dodgers, you, me, and
Joe, and argue over who was gonna catch the foul ball? Ruth,
you look fabulous, you really do. But if you don't stop smoking,
I'm going to tell your mother, never mind she's dead and in her
grave God rest her soul. Harry, I swear to God the funniest
thing I ever saw was you trying to run out of the bunkhouse
with your feet stuck to the floor. Dear sweet Miriam. Maker
of the best challah second only to my wife's, of course, because
she'll kill me if I don't say that and then we'd have to go ahead
with the original purpose of this gathering which was to celebrate my death. Well, not celebrate I suppose. Not my death.
But to gather in my memory. And that is where I shall keep
you all. In my memory, which is close to my heart. Anatomy's
a funny thing, isn't it?"

So then I sit down. I don't want to look at anyone, but
I know someone's gonna think something's wrong if I don't
look somewhere, so I turn and there's Miriam so I look at her.
Miriam, I hear myself talking.

"Miriam, you were so beautiful when you were young. So
beautiful it made me ache to look at you. My god you were
beautiful."

She shifts in her seat. I'm making her uncomfortable.

"That was a long time ago, Sal," she says and she makes it

sound like something happened between us which it never did. Not then. Not later. Not ever. Not that I didn't want it to. But Louis woulda killed me, then and now.

"Yes," I tell her. "It was. A long time ago. And now we're old and ugly."

She tells me to stop it or she's leaving.

Alluva sudden I'm wondering where Maxie is.

"I'm right here, Sal," she says, like I said it out loud which I'm sure I didn't. She's standing behind me. I catch sight of her in the mirror across the room. She's looking at Miriam. Comparing herself, I'll bet you. She's a year younger than Miriam. In the mirror, there's a hundred people between us.

"You're beautiful like always, Maxie," I tell her.

"I'm old and ugly," she says, "just like you said."

"I wasn't talking about you," I tell her. "I was talking about me."

And this is when the doorbell buzzer sounds and Henry Rivers who's the pharmacist Maxie's been going to since she refused to have anything to do with Laura and who she corralled into being the doorman for this event opens the door.

You know how they say when you're drowning you see your whole life pass between your eyes? I guess I am in a manner of speaking drowning because that's exactly what happens when Henry answers that buzzer. I see the bars of my playpen, and my mother rolling out noodles on the dining room table, I see the spinning top I got for Christmas when I couldn'ta been more than three, I see the desk I sat in fourth grade with "Maury" carved across the top so whenever I tried to write neat there were holes in my paper where the pencil poked through the groove Maury made who knows how many years before. I see Ebbets Field and the back of the head of a big guy who sat in front of me the day PeeWee Reese tripled in the bottom of the ninth. I see the induction center where I loaned myself to Uncle Sam and the jungle where I thought sure I'd leave my rotting yellow feet. I see Jones Beach with Maxie and Miriam and Laura sitting side by side on a beach towel and Louis and Joe standing behind them, posing for a snapshot. I see Freddy when he was just a baby still in the hospital and Louis was still handing out the cigars that I wish I had one of now, and Miriam at Freddy's wedding dancing the *hora* like nobody's business, and Joe got so drunk they hadda load him in a cab and send him home because Laura hadda keep the store open and said he should be the one to go to the wedding because he knew Louis and Miriam the longest. I see the gondolier in Venice that sang to us on our twentieth anniversary and told us he'd pray for us to have kids like we coulda dealt with kids by that time in our lives. I see my father may he rest in peace how proud he looked at my first communion and the time he taught me to drive and then took me out for my first beer and told me what he called "da factsa da bees and boids" and all at the same time I see him how he looked just before he died and I finally had the nerve to tell him I love him. I see my mother the way she'd wave her walking stick at me when she wanted to remind me how old and weak she was. I see Joe and Laura the day I sold the baseball card and told 'em what I wanted to do.

I see Laura, ohmygod for real. She's standing in the doorway, holding her little pocketbook and a manila envelope. She's standing there. No, I mean for real. For really real. This is no hallucination of a crazy old man.

I see her see Maxie, but she doesn't see me. I see Maxie see her. Maxie's heading toward the door. Laura's waiting for her. Now they're talking.

From here I can't tell what they're saying, but Laura's giving Maxie the envelope. Now they're stepping outside.

Alluva sudden it comes clear to me what's going on. It's the policy. Laura thinks I'm dead. She doesn't realize I'm still here. She thinks I'm dead. She read about the memorial and figured I went through with it and now she's giving Maxie the insurance policy. Ohmigod.

Miriam's eyes aren't as sharp as they used to be.

"Is that Laura?" she asks Louis. Louis says it looks like it to him.

He looks at me and says "God almighty, Sal, you look like you just saw a ghost."

It was my ghost, I tell him. He doesn't know what I'm talking about.

I'm still staring at the door. I didn't want Maxie to know. I knew she wouldn't understand. I don't know what I'm gonna say to her now. What the hell can I say to her? That it was the only way I knew how to make sure she'd never have to give up the house? That we just didn't have enough money for me to take a long time to die? That I was tired? Afraid of pain? And here's the crazy part. That I didn't even take the stuff Laura gave me? That I didn't even have the nerve when it came right down to it to die in dignity?

That when they took me to the hospital, I thought God was gonna let me off the hook and I wouldn't have to do it myself? And then when Maxie said we're gonna celebrate, how could I?

There's a scream from outside and Henry jumps up to open the door. There's Laura hugging Maxie and yelling "Thanks God, where is he?" And Maxie points to me across the room and Laura comes racing through the tables with everyone looking at her wondering what she's doing here 'cause they all

know how Maxie feels about the Porters now and she gets to
me and throws her arms around my neck, almost knocks me
over in my chair; I'm too surprised to stand up and greet her
like a gentleman should. "Sal Thanks God" she's crying in my
ear and I can smell that faint smell on her of the pharmacy,
the pills and the ointments. Maxie's right behind her holding
the envelope and crying.

All our friends, our neighbors, our acquaintances, even the
waiters, a hundred or more, bless their hearts, are pretending
nothing's happening. They'll watch us in the mirror and ask
Miriam later.

"God, Maxie, I'm sorry, I didn't want you to end up..." I
almost say like Laura but I catch myself.

Speaking of Laura, she's crying. "I thought I killed you,"
she says.

And Maxie's crying too, and telling me *she's* sorry.

"Good God, Maxie, why should you be sorry?"

She says she didn't realize how much Joe's trouble affected
me and she's sorry she was so sneaky about it but when she
found those pills she had to change them and then she was
afraid she was being punished for being selfish and wanting
me to live when I got so sick anyway and she never suspected
it was about the insurance and why was I so worried about
money anyway..."

I interrupt her. "You knew about the pills?"

"I didn't—I found them when I was putting your socks
away," she says. "You know the heavy ones I always put in the
back of your sock drawer, and there they were. I couldn't help
seeing them and it wasn't anything you already take so I took
one to Henry and he told me what they were and I had him
make me some sugar pills that looked the same..."

I'm laughing. That worries her. "Maxie," I say, "I never took them anyway. I was too chicken. I was a big chicken, Maxie, I was too afraid to die."

Now Laura's laughing too. Crying and laughing at the same time. "Only the top four were real anyway," she says. "I knew you'd suspect something if you didn't feel anything at all from them, so I only gave you four real ones. I was hoping it'd be just enough to scare you and make you realize you want to live after all. So your trip to the hospital..."

"Was just the natural course of events," I say.

Maxie's looking at me. "I'm not ready for you to go yet, Sal," she says.

"Apparently I'm not ready to go yet either," I say. "And I get the feeling that it wouldn't matter anyway because there's a conspiracy to keep me alive."

"Is that okay?" Maxie wants to know. What a question!

"It's been a lot of years," I say. "Aren't you sick of me yet?" Uh oh, she's crying again. "You ruined my plan," I tell her. "You and Laura both. Now how am I gonna provide for you when I'm dead and gone for real? The policy's up for renewal in two months and I don't have any baseball cards left."

"Baseball cards?"

"I had a collection. I sold the last one to pay for the policy."

"I never knew you had a baseball card collection."

"I know."

"Well, don't you worry about it anyway. I got a little saved away."

"You got what?"

"A little saved away. A savings account. It's enough to pay the premium. It's more than enough."

"Since when is this you got a savings account?"

"Since before we were married. Fifty-three years, you wanna know exactly."

"I never knew that."

"Now you know."

Louis, bless his heart, can tell it's time for this party to wind up. He's been listening, he and Miriam. Discreetly, of course.

"Maxie," he says, "may I say a few words of farewell to the guests so you can get on home?"

Maxie nods.

"Folks," he lifts his glass. "One more toast for the road," he says. He's good like that. Like they didn't know it was time to go, but now they know. The women are all reaching for their purses, even while they hold up their glasses. Except Miriam. She's looking at us with a big smile on her face. Oh, you bet she's gonna enjoy telling this one.

"To friendship," Louis says, "and to marriage. We send our dear friends Sal and Maxie home now," and he does that little pause so we should know something poetic is about to be said, "'two by two in the ark of/ the ache of it' to know they are cherished by all of us here, and to continue to celebrate their lives together, thankful that we have come here not to bury Sal, but to praise him. Good night, friends." He downs the champagne and leans over to whisper in Miriam's ear. "Denise Levertov." She smiles up at him as he helps her up from the table. They're cute together. He's a lucky guy, that Louis. So am I.

"Let's walk home," I say. "It'll be good exercise. Good for my Program. We can pick the car up later."

Miriam offers to drive it home for us. Louis will follow her, and she'll leave the key under the front mat on the passenger side.

"Laura," Maxie says, "you want to join us? We have some catching up to do."

Our friends are all filtering out into the night. Laura is saying hello and goodbye to The Other Louie, Harry, Ruth,

and Mary. They hadn't any of them seen her since the indict-
ment. She tells them Joe's doing all right. They expect him to
get a suspended sentence due to his age and previously spot-
less record including coaching Little League all those years and
organizing the Grafton Avenue food bank. Plans are being
made for a get together, including Joe. Across the room, Maxie
finds the head caterer, gives him a tip to distribute and final
instructions for locking up.

There's an ache. It feels pretty good, if you want to know
the truth.

The Persistence of Memory

ONCE YOU LEARN you never forget. Marie could hear the voice of her father, encouraging her to pick herself and her new Schwinn bike up from the pavement and try again. He'd refused to put training wheels on it, though her mother had fretted about that. Instead, he'd hold the bike, and run alongside until the speed exceeded his ability to keep up. Then he'd shout encouraging words at his pigtailed and petrified daughter until she fell over. Backpedal! Brake! You can do it! Stop and slide off the seat! Get your feet off the pedals and on the ground!

Bruise by bruise, scrape by scrape, Marie had mastered the art of staying upright, backpedaling to apply the coaster brakes and slow down, sliding from the seat at exactly the same moment the bicycle came to a full stop. She'd even gotten to the point where she could ride hands-free and, inspired by her favorite circus act, sidesaddle. She could balance another child on her handlebars and did so with each of her three younger siblings until they, too, had gotten their own first bikes.

So it was with absolute confidence in her muscle memory and abilities that Marie confronted her great-granddaughter's bicycle, kept in the garage for Celia's occasional visits. She'd been told she was too old to be on the road, and her license was taken away. Not by the state, mind you, but by her own child. Her son Matt had actually hidden it from her. He knew she was too crafty not to have a spare key, and he knew she was a stickler for obeying the law. Without that, she wouldn't dare take her Hyundai into traffic. California had no problems with her abilities: they'd issued her most recent license good through her hundred-and-first birthday.

It's not that she drove much anyway. She just wanted to go down to the Market Cafe to have a little lunch on the balcony with Amy. They had a senior special she'd been enjoying every Tuesday for the past twenty-seven years. Her forays to this favored spot had outlasted even the original owners of the place. A series of new owners had taken it over. Waitresses and waiters had come and gone, menus had changed, but there had always been a senior special at lunch and she always had it on Tuesday.

Her oldest friends gathered there with her at first, but one by one they shed their mortal coils and shuffled off into the Great Beyond. Marie began eating lunch with their children. Now, she was on her way to meet the newly retired granddaughter of a woman Marie had called her very best friend in eighth grade. Shirley had married young, bred young, so her daughter Ella had been only sixteen years younger than Shirley. Ella kept the family tradition going and now her daughter Amy was 65 with great-grandchildren of her own. Marie liked Amy. She had spunk. It would be fun to see Amy at lunch, to catch up on her plans for retirement. If Amy was a bike rider, maybe they could take a spin now and then together, do a picnic or something.

Matt had come for a few days to visit and talk her into doing things his way. Having secreted her proof of road-worthiness, he insisted she alert him when she needed a ride, so she could see how nice it would be to move into the Living Well Retirement Home where you never had to fight traffic because they have a little bus that took residents to all the malls and movies. Well she would be damned if she was going to start acting like some rich woman with a chauffeur just because she was looking at the near edge of a century. And she was not moving. Don't let them carry me out of here, she'd instructed her next-door neighbor, unless they're carrying me to Forest Lawn.

Marie stood for a brief moment contemplating the bike. In her day, you got black ones or blue ones. This bicycle was hot pink and metallic lavender. Her great-grandsons had black, red, silver, or blue bikes. All the fuss over what were boy colors and girl colors didn't make sense to Marie.

She remembered how to tilt it and lift a leg up and through to straddle the center bar. Another thing she didn't understand. Why aren't all bikes this easy to mount? The fellas always have to risk—if not life and limb—something maybe even more important to get themselves all the way up there on the seat, and god forbid they slip off. She remembered Matt's first such mishap vividly, and she bet he remembered it even more.

Taking the helmet from where it had hung on the handlebars, putting it on, pulling the strap tight, Marie felt ready for anything. She pushed off, wobbled out of the garage and down the driveway. She turned right onto the road. Market Cafe was a straight shot down a mild hill, about a mile ahead, just past the intersection on the left.

In no time at all she found her secure balance. It was surprisingly easy to pedal. You're right, Pop, she called cheerily, picking up speed. You never forget! She rested her legs, letting the momentum of wheels on downhill asphalt take her forward.

Oh, the joy of wind on the face! How long had it been? Decades, but how many now? Matt would have been about twelve when he got too old to want to be seen riding in the company of his mother and father. Then Roger wasn't able to enjoy bicycling anymore because his knee kicked up too much. Marie had given all the bikes away when they moved to their GI-loan backed new house.

At the halfway point she lifts her hands into the air, just for a second or two. Yes! She can still do it! They want her to move into a home. Pshaw! When she says it in company, they mock her for her old-fashioned speech. Here on the open empty road, she shouts it out. PSHAW! I can take care of myself! She pedals harder, picks up speed.

Her Schwinn was a black 24-incher. She'd begged for it one Christmas and been given to understand in no uncertain terms that it was a luxury the family simply couldn't afford. Yet there it stood, on Christmas morning, the surprise of the century. It had lasted a good long time, too, and a lucky thing. When the Depression hit, she rode that bike everywhere, and having it allowed her to search far and wide for the job she finally found ten miles from home, clerking three days a week in a department store.

She coasts downhill past a clump of serviceberries. She never sees them when she's driving past, but now they jump out at her, inviting her to stop on the way back and pick enough for a jar of jam.

Approaching the intersection now, she backpedals to slow down. The pedals offer no resistance. The bike speeds on. Pop, how the hell do you stop this thing? No pigtails now, just pure panic. And coming from the left on the crossroad, a mammoth semi. On she zooms, clutching the rubber handlebar grips, unaware that the braking system she so desperately wants is a mere inch from her white knuckles.

If she's lucky, the truck will skedaddle right on through and get out of the way. Then she can survive the intersection and aim for the grass in front of the cafe. That's bound to slow her down at least a little! But the truck, too, is slowing down, preparing to turn.

She barrels on. Dammit, she yells. I want to celebrate my hundredth!

Some ancient part of her mind heeds the call. While her conscious mind holds on for dear life, the feral brain makes a series of crucial decisions. Lean to the left, turn the wheel, register the horrified look on the part of the truck driver, narrowly miss the collision, correct for leaning too far to the left, oh no! Another, steeper downhill now. No one coming? No one coming. U turn! Stabilize! Breathe!

At last she feels the bicycle begin to slow down. Pedal. Steady. She barks the command at her hands and miraculously, they obey. Ease over to the edge of the road, ready for one last turn into the cafe parking lot. A car ahead. You can do it. Remember to signal your turn this time. Steady!

She hits the curb and the bike, surprised by the sudden change of terrain, skids sideways and bucks her into the drainage ditch that runs along the driveway, her skirt immodestly askew. The bike falls back into the path of the oncoming motorist.

A crunch. The squeal of brakes, voices shouting, hubbub aplenty.

Her hip hurts, but whose wouldn't? Otherwise, everything seems to be working. The crowd reaches her just as she's about to stand up.

Don't try to move! Stay right there! Hold still! An ambulance is on the way!

Oh for goodness sake, cancel it, she insists, and hauls herself up out of the cattails, dripping muddy water. The bike, alas, is mangled beyond rideability, but she is miraculously unscathed. No, she is fine, really, and about to be late. The skirt's a mess, but it will dry. She'll take the outside steps to the balcony so she won't track dirt through the cafe.

After lunch, she calls Matt for a ride home. He bellows and fumes, fusses and grumbles. Could have been killed! Crazy old lady! Retirement home! Blah blah blah blah blah.

Well if you won't let me drive, what choice do I have?

Fine. Fine! If you want to kill yourself go ahead. Just don't say I didn't try to drum some sense into your ancient contrarian head. He slaps the license down on the table.

The next day she drives to the bicycle shop to pick out a replacement for the one she totaled. Matt goes along, begrudgingly acknowledging that her skills as a driver are consummate. Well, "adequate" is actually the word he's willing to part with. At least, he grouses, you'll have a seatbelt on the next time you run into something.

They pick out a new shiny bike for Celia, purple and glittery. While she pays for it, Matt browses the accessories, giving Marie an opportunity to chat up the nice young sales clerk. So, sonny, she says, how exactly do you stop one of these?

About the Author

JAN MAHER lives and writes in the Pioneer Valley of Massachusetts. Her novel *Heaven, Indiana* was named a *Kirkus* Best of 2018. A companion work, *Earth As It Is,* was named to *Kirkus* Best Indies of 2017 and won the 2018 American Fiction Award in the LGBT category. Her plays include *Widow's Walk,* which gained finalist status in the Actors Theatre of Louisville Ten-Minute Play Contest, *Most Dangerous Women, Intruders and Ismene.* Her poetry, short fiction, and essays have appeared in literary journals and anthologies. She is a Senior Scholar at the Institute for Ethics in Public Life, State University of New York at Plattsburgh.

Made in the USA
Middletown, DE
18 February 2020

84882319R00078